The Holidays Bring Stress, Comfort, Mystery, and, in the End, Ginger-Flavored Joy.

Boxing Day at Wentworth Manor brings joy and celebration. But a cruel crime threatens to ruin the party.

A Christmas parade, a mug full of comfort, and a special new friend help a mother learn how to better show her love.

Walt knows y'all think Santa Claus ain't real. One snowy Christmas Eve, Walt learns better.

The Christmas season hits hard for some people. Yet it sometimes also brings hope for recovery and renewal.

Stuart's Stop 'N Shop, always open, even for Christmas. Then the holiday spirit surprises Stuart, Bobby, and Pete.

When the Santa Train fails to make the trip, one special person makes all the difference for a grateful town.

When the magic of Old Christmas makes an appearance, the magic of music turns sadness to joy.

If there's one thing entrepreneur Tina Braddock knows, it's that a good salesperson rolls with the unexpected. Even when the unexpected only stands four inches tall.

Carrie faces Christmas in a new city, far from those who refuse to see her. Then she finds a true family to join for the celebration.

Ellie faces unwelcome changes in her life, threatening her Christmas spirit. Only Deke, Miss Pebbles, and a pan of Grammy's gingerbread promise a joyful new start.

More great reads from Jason A. Adams

www.JasonAdamsBooks.com

Novellas:

Agonist

Collections and Anthologies:

Normally Fantastic

On the Case!

Capeless Heroes

Through the Squirrel Tree

Tales From the Squirrel Garden: Volume 1

(with Kari Kilgore)

Partnership in Crime

Shadows Mountain Deep

Partners in Romance

Near Future Forward

JASON A. ADAMS

Winter Delights

A Joyful Collection Full of Holiday Cheer

Spiral Publishing, Ltd.

Winter Delights: A Joyful Collection Full of Holiday Cheer

To all of you. May your holiday season be full of laughter and good company.

CONTENTS

FROM THE BRAIN SQUIRRELS
HOLIDAY SHIPPING DEPOT

Who doesn't love a good holiday?

Especially those holidays that fall right around the Winter Solstice. Whether it's Christmas, Hanukkah, Kwanzaa, Festivus, Soyal, Ōmisoka, or the dozens of specialized family and community festivals scattered across the globe, that last couple of weeks of December has a little something for everybody.

Being a guy who likes writing happy and/or heartwarming stories (my heart at least, your mileage may vary), I've written scads of holiday stories over the years. Being a guy raised where and how I was, that usually means Christmas of the Santa and Frosty variety. So most of the stories you'll find here are centered around that tradition.

Not all, though. I grew up bouncing around the

country and globe as an Air Force draftee, so I saw several different ways to celebrate the turning of Winter. As an adult living in the massive melting pot of Atlanta, I learned several more.

After moving back to the ancestral mountains of my Appalachian forbearers, I started taking all those experiences, adding in people I've met and stories I've heard, giving them all a good, hard stirring, and writing down what my Brain Squirrels handed back to me.

There are no unhappy endings in this collection of ten holiday-themed stories. There are a couple of poignant endings, ones that still put a little sand in my eye when I read them (and I *wrote* the dang things), and some that leave the characters in a more hopeful place than they started in.

Most, of course, are happy endings. It's that time of year, after all.

First on the list is "Ballerinas and Super Cats," set on Boxing Day in a grand old mansion full of grand old tradition, and featuring a couple of four-legged crime stoppers who save the day. While the kitties are based on our own furry freeloaders, Clark and Kent are better at the whole helpful thing.

Next, we head to Las Vegas for "The Healing Power of Atole," where a lonely woman learns about *Las Posadas* and how much good company and good beverages can cure family relationships, and help create new ones.

"If I'm Lyin' I'm Dyin'" is an Appalachian tall tale told by an old-timer who absolutely believes what he's saying. Walt's here to tell you everything you thought you knew about Santa and how he delivers goodies is all wrong.

Chuck's world has shrunk down quite a bit in "The Twelve Steps of Christmas," a story about small joys and small improvements for a man doing his best to clean up the wreckage he left behind. Honesty, hard work, and a willingness to accept what's offered help make this Christmas the best he's had in a long time.

I write a lot about found family, those people you make an important part of your life by choice, not because of shared DNA. Atlanta is full of found families, and we meet one of them in "A Convenience Store Christmas," where Santas wear aprons and sling a mean barbecue.

"Long May it Ring" takes us back to the Appalachians, where The Santa Train runs every year, except one. The Santa Train is a very real thing, although I've set this story a fair bit before the tradition actually started. But I love a good folk story, and with fiction I get to set the rules however I want, so there.

Staying in Appalachia, we meet Richard Tolliver in the here and now, though neither we nor Richard stay there. One of the old traditions here is Old Christmas, which people in the rest of the world know as Epiphany, January 6. One of the more obscure traditions around Old Christmas is called "Breaking Up Christmas," which is something I'd love to see come back.

Taking a break from the more emotional stories, we next travel back to the Las Vegas valley with "Elves and Ergonomics," where an office-furniture designer gets the strangest order she never could have expected. Anyone who works for themselves know that you take the commissions where they come, and never say no.

"A True Family Holiday" returns us to Atlanta and another found family, all helping each other through their various holidays with nothing but acceptance, joy, and the knowledge that none of us have to be alone.

The last story, also set in Appalachia, turned out much more like a holiday romance movie than I expected when I first sat down to write. The setting of "Ginger Magic" is a small town fair by and for the native redheads, celebrating their love of all things ginger.

So put on your warmest stockings, grab a mug of

your favorite hot chocolate, eggnog, or coquito (spiked or not), and settle in the softest easy chair by the fire. Everyone in here would love to meet you and tell you their stories.

And who knows? Maybe invite you to join their families.

WINTER DELIGHTS

JASON A. ADAMS
Author of Dirk Knight: The Case of the Rustled Ranch
Ballerinas and
Super Cats

For all those who love at will.

1

WHO NEEDS cops when you have The Amazing Super Cats?

And if Cal didn't hustle his butt on back to the Big House with this ridiculously heavy bag of kibble, his toes might freeze before his arms fell off, and the Super Cats would take their cruel, horrible revenge.

They'd yowl and cry like the nigh-starveling refugees they were, squeezing their guts between his legs and falling to the floor in their fainting weakness.

The evening rated a slow stroll instead of full bustle, though. Wentworth Avenue was dolled up just perfectly for the big Boxing Day celebration at Wentworth House.

He walked through the historic district, past Wentworth Haberdashery, Wentworth Millinery, Wentworth Carriage Repair.

This last was partly interpretational, partly a working carriage house used to repair the estate's classic vehicles. Cal had spent every free minute he could drag away from directing operations at the big house hanging around the place. And the smithy down the alley where they worked metal black, white, and red.

That reminded him. He needed to do a few more reps on the curling bar with his left arm. His right was getting a little too out of whack from the hammer.

He slowed down by Wentworth Cakes and Ale. They'd locked up early, of course. Everyone would be at the Boxing Day shindig. But he could still catch a whiff of apple pie, peach tart, and candied walnuts sneaking out through the door jamb.

Good thing he walked most of his shopping. The C&A had a siren's song he couldn't resist.

The lovely antique (ish) wrought-iron (looking) streetlamps cast a soft, buttery glow from their triple globes. Through the ribbed and leaded glass (plexi), the clusters of colored LED bulbs stayed dutifully tuned to that warm, olden light.

Later on in the week, they'd be set to a rotating rainbow of color, washing the street in that good ol' holiday cheer for the rest of the Twelve Days.

A light snow had fallen that morning, covering

the little mountain town of Sabre Creek in five inches of gorgeous fluff. A nice warmish snow, too, so all the trees and hedges wore their coats of white like so many frosted mini-wheats.

Or like camouflaged soldiers of the 10th Light Infantry, preparing to scale the Reisa Pass during Operation...

Cal shook his head. No matter what else might change, he'd never stop being a nerd. Which was fine and dandy. He might be Calvin Isaiah Wentworth V, but these days the family patriarch preferred multi-faceted dice, a good comic, and an excellent treatise on military structures of the Gallic Wars to anything as mundane as running the family's namesake textile mills.

Not that any of the Wentworth Mills were in Wentworth hands anymore. Not since CW3 and his penchant for buying dodgy stocks and too much brandy in the years before the crash of '29.

Grandma Irene had to sell just about everything after CW3 lost his mills and gave a double-barrel to a piece of his mind, but she'd found enough help to let her stay in the old house until she passed away just after midnight on New Year's Day, 2000. The old gal was an interesting piece of work, but she'd made it into her third century, and how many people got to say that?

He paused across from the manor's intricate black gates to let one of the jingling horse-drawn sleighs pull in. He crossed the street and took a moment to admire the original hand-hammered wrought-iron ivy and flowers that twined through stout bars, turning this many-hundred-pound barrier into a light and airy piece of fairy-tale beauty.

Admiring the gates also gave the horses a bit more time to pull away. He'd been to the stables, even worked up the guts to give Clyde—a mammoth (what else?) Clydesdale that made him feel like an ant—a sugar cube from his palm.

Cal flexed his fingers, still glad they were all there, and walked toward the brightly lit and freshly painted columns of the manor's grand façade.

His attention split time between watching for the occasional horse apple and drinking in the sight of Wentworth Manor, all dressed up and ready for the evening's forty guests and benefactors.

An oversized frosted cupcake of a Victorian, complete with round tower and cupola, sat behind what should have been a completely out of place antebellum-style entrance. Somehow, the original architect had made it work, and Wentworth Manor had been written up in journals far and wide as one of the earliest fusion-concept domiciles in the Mid-Atlantic region.

Wide, granite steps swept upward in twin, narrowing curves to a broad planked rocking chair platform. Four waist-thick simple Doric columns, all cut and smoothed from the trunk of the same single hoary old Eastern Chestnut. All coated with traditional sparkly limewash expertly applied by Larry Bowdre, an old fart who'd been working the grounds since Grandma Irene still put on her dancing shoes from time to time.

A couple of college kids in black tailcoats and blinding white vests and shirts so starched the cured lime on the columns had competition stood to either side of the twin eight-foot-tall studded oak doors, bowing butlerly as party guests climbed the stairs and wafted inside. The one on the right—Jack? Jake? —broke character long enough to steady a woman with Professional Soccer Mom hair and a truly horrible tracksuit in magenta and velvet who stumbled on the marble threshold stone, which hadn't settled as deeply as the wooden bits around it.

Cal made a mental note to thank the kid for asking PSM to put the selfie-stick away in her duffel-sized sequined purse (magenta) and watch her feet instead.

No grand entryway for Cal, however. He scooted around the side of the big stairs to the service entrance on the left. Nowhere near as large and fancy, but this door opened straight into the kitchen, itself bigger than many apartments Cal had graced, and filled with gleaming swathes of modern stainless steel instead of the period pieces in the rest of the manor.

He stepped inside into the frenetic, highly organized chaos of the annual Boxing Day Blast.

Fifteen men and women wearing whites which matched or contrasted with their skin, with hair of every color natural or bottled, milled around like moths in a high wind, rattling them pots and pans and whipping up a huge mouth-watering venison roast, tureens of bisques and purees, loaves of crusty bread slowly risen over three days.

He might outdo the cats on nigh-starvation.

"Thank *goodness* you're finally here!" Cal saw a curly cascade of fiery red over the top of his kibble bag as throaty mezzo-soprano tones set his belly a-quiver. "You've only got ten minutes to get your Lord of the Manor on."

Hair and voice belonged to Katy Braun, his assistant director and talent manager. And everything else that required real organizational skill. Cal was a great numbers guy and kept the books tidy as a pin, but without Katy he'd have to lock the doors and send everyone home.

Assuming he could find the key, of course.

"Hey, Katy," he said, walking over to drop the cat food by their feeder in the corner. "Yeah, it'll just take me a sec—shit!"

Unlike Madame Soccer Mom, Cal couldn't watch his feet with his arms full of kitty slops. So of course one of the Super Cats had picked the perfect time to play roadblock.

The nasal, scratchy squawk of dudgeon told him Clark the Twenty Pound Chonk had done the honors this time. Kent, his slightly smaller tuxedo twin came meyowling right behind, clearly nigh-starved and wilting from hunger, rubbing greedily against Cal's leg.

"Useless little..." Cal decided to set the bag down by the wall instead. Hard to play Señor Calvin Isaiah Wentworth with his neck in a brace.

"Tsk. Such language, Master Wentworth." Katy smiled, checking her watch. "Dinner's on schedule, and all your *servants* are awaiting your generosity. So go on, git! I'll feed the Dynamic Duo."

"That's Batman and Robin," he called over his shoulder. "Clark Kent doesn't—"

A damp dishrag hit the back of his head, so he decided to wait on the rest of the explanation.

2

———

NINE MINUTES LATER, Cal hustled down the servant's stairs, far narrower and way more plain-utilitarian than the grand staircase of the great hall.

The butler's uniform fit better this year than last. All the shopping walks had done more good than the C&A could counteract, thank goodness.

He looked down at his wrist to check his cufflinks. Good thing, too.

"Jesus, Clark. Go find a mouse or something."

Super Chonk sprawled along a step about halfway down; feet, tail, and gut hanging over the edge as he licked his whiskers and stared up at this plebian interloper in his domain.

"Get a job, cat." But Cal reached to scrub a head larger than his fist as he continued toward the great hall. Katy should be...

And there she was. Dressed in her black and white maid's uniform to match his own servant garb.

She was scanning the crowd and sneaking peeks at her anachronistic smartwatch, probably wondering just where the hell her boss was.

He stepped up beside her and gently bumped her elbow with his. She saw him and relaxed, but not before giving him her best matronly scowl as she straightened the white bowtie he'd insisted on tying himself. Badly. She'd mastered the loving tie-straighten, and liked to use it in her role as Mrs. Elizabeth Wentworth, nee Stockton, young English bride of CW1.

As if great-great-gramps had ever been that lucky.

In the great hall, three generations of Wentworths, including an incredibly young Grandma Irene, stared disapprovingly at the crowd from their canvas prisons around the upstairs gallery. Electric versions of gas lights lit everything with a not-too-bright ambience, with strategic mini-spots highlighting the portraits, maps, and sketches of the family mill.

Guests milled around, sipping champagne and spiced cider as Ben, their chief interpreter, filled the time with facts about the Wentworths and their manor.

"When Calvin Wentworth the Third tragically passed away just at the start of the Great Depression, his wife and only heir Irene, who was with child at the time, had no choice but to sell the house and grounds. Selena Holland, matriarch of the Sabre Creek DAR, had a love for the history of Sabre Creek, and agreed to purchase the estate in trust, ensuring Mrs. Wentworth could live out her days in the home, surrounded by all the things familiar and dear to her. In fact, upstairs we'll see Mrs. Wentworth's boudoir and drawing room, restored to their original furnishings and décor of 1875, when the first Mrs. Wentworth—"

A little sugar-coated, but that was all right. Grandma Irene gave up the house, but the terms of the agreement meant she got to die in bed (and the DAR probably hadn't expected she'd outlive 'em all), and her take from the estate's income let her live a comfortable life, and leave a good starting stake to her grandchildren.

No more Wentworth fortune, but Cal hadn't started his adulthood nearly as nigh-starved as Clark and Kent tried to be.

Ms. Holland had an almost religious love of the town's past that put Cal's own historical interest to shame. When Wentworth Manor went on the block in 1930, she'd written letters, sent telegrams, made speeches all across four states, all but begging for funds from her patriotic sisters.

And she'd beaten the bank man to the signing table with more than enough to purchase the manor house, all contents and outbuildings, plus the five acres enclosed by the original brick wall.

Grandma Irene had liked to complain about being a guest in her own home, but she and Selena had stayed friends over the years. In fact, one of the few non-1875 pieces in her bedroom upstairs was a beautiful clockwork ballerina carved from narwhal ivory and enshrined in a crystal ball on the mantel. Some elder Holland had brought it back from some sea slaughter or other, and presented it to his wife. Who passed it down to Ms. Holland.

Who gave it to her poor widowed friend. Purely for friendship's sake, of course.

Cal had been fighting the museum board on including in the tours the little tidbit that Ms. Holland was a *very* frequent overnight guest of the house, and often traveled abroad with Grandma Irene. The Sister-Betty-Better'n-Yous in town had talked behind their hands, but both women were too well-loved in the town for more than a few tongues to wag.

The tight friendship they shared just might

explain the engraving on the bottom of the ballerina globe.

To my fair I., the most wonderful person I have ever known. This pretty dancer will long be dust before your beauty fades in my eyes. S.

Sadly, Ms. Holland had passed away when Cal was only five and he didn't remember her all that well. His dad, CW4, never said anything, but Cal doubted it had been much of a secret in the family.

Especially since Grandma Irene's clothes went from bright and bouncy to somber and plain after the funeral. And for all her perky, good-natured snark when she had company, Cal remembered seeing her winding the ballerina when she thought she was alone, using a tiny silver key she wore around her neck and never removed.

Watching the timeless dancer twirl and spin while her heart leaked from her eyes.

3

———————

A SQUALL FROM upstairs shook Cal from his woolgathering. Some guest had discovered a Super Cat, probably right where he wasn't supposed to be.

Jake—yep, Jake, not Jack—gave the drive a look-over, made sure no stragglers lurked, then he and his partner shut the massive doors. Jake took hold of a hanging velvet rope and gave it a tug, sending a deep brazen bong bonging through the house.

Cal sometimes snuck and yanked the rope after hours, when he was the only one left inside. He *loved* that thing. Had since he was knee high to a grasshopper.

He and Katy went to stand in the middle of the thick pile of the replica Persian rug in the center of the hall. The original, which had more than a little wear and was pretty thin from over a century of

15

assorted feet, Wentworth and non-, was now on display in the Highlands Regional Textile Museum out by the old millworks.

All forty guests came chattering down the grand staircase, half of them with hand on rail and Scarlett O'Hara in their eyes.

Sheesh. Big or not, it was just a staircase. But then, they hadn't grown up pelting up and down the silly thing with their cousins.

Herding the guests along came Jake, his butler partner (and that kid was a last-minute replacement whose name had fallen right out of Cal's head), and a couple of housemaids in outfits matching Katy's—excuse me, Mrs. Wentworth's—own.

Once everyone was spread in a rough arc in front of the staircase, Cal held up his hands for quiet and dredged up his Veddy Propah voice.

"Ladies and Gentlemen. I want you to know how pleased we of the household are that you have taken time from your busy lives to join us here at Wentworth Manor for what my dear Elizabeth and I consider our most important celebration."

The four "servants" stepped forward, and Katy handed each either a folded frock coat, or a vintagey lace shawl.

"On this day, the day after Christmas, Boxing Day, my wife tells me that in the land of her birth, her family's custom was not only to send their servants home with boxes of good cheer to share with their families, but also before the leave-taking, to allow *us* the honor of serving *them*."

Cell phones raised on high and flashes flashed as Jake and the others removed jackets and aprons, donning the long black frock coats and pretty shawls. The men bowed to Cal and Katy, the women curtseyed nicely.

"Now then, it is my pleasure to request your company in the dining hall, where my dear Lizzie the Maid and I, Wentworth the Butler, shall serve you and our loyal staff the finest fare to be had between here and never-gonna-get-there!"

Cal raised his arms as the guests cheered and applauded, then bowed and swept his arm toward the correct door as Jake and his cronies led the way to the gut-buster, clicking the red counter in his hand as each guest passed and watching for stragglers.

"Whew! Almost done," Katy said, wiping a melodramatic wrist across her not-at-all-sweaty forehead. "Come help me slop the hogs, my darling husband?"

Cal could think of a lot better ways to spend time with Katy, but a life of gaming and Management of Historical Family Dwellings hadn't left him with a working asker-outer. One of these days he'd—

"Shit," he said, showing the red plastic click-counter to Katy. "Only thirty-nine. Who the hell is missing?"

"Damn," Katy said, finger bobbing as she counted heads around the sixteen-foot-long mahogany table. Not so easy given the squabble between her own height and the towering candelabras and piles of goodies all along the board.

"No time," Cal said. "You go on in. Draft one of the kitcheneers to help serve. Tell them I came down with a sudden attack of the vapours or whatever, but I should return once my constitution blah-blah. I'll go check the rooms."

Katy nodded, straightened the stupid tie again, and dashed around the corner to the breakfast room's door into the kitchen.

Cal quickly made the downstairs circuit. Didn't take long. Like most big houses of the era, every room opened on each adjacent one, meaning a careful jogger could get his laps in without ever crossing his own path.

Nothing. He should probably check the cameras, but he'd wait on that until he knew for sure Number Forty wasn't in the house anymore. Besides, maybe whoever it was just had to take a leak.

Up the grand staircase, keeping to the right side where the bannister was more sturdy and the stairs didn't squeak as much, a quick duck down the servant and guest wing to check the bedrooms.

No one in there.

"I do beg your pardon," he called in his best LoM boom. "I must insist you join the party below. Everyone wishes to have your opinion of the stuffed quail."

Nothing.

Hm.

He glanced in the Matron's Room, Grandma Irene's restored bedroom.

Nothing disturbed on the big canopied four-poster. All the protective display covers still in place over the dressing table and porcelain wash basin and pitcher. Nothing missing from the—

Wait.

Where the hell was Grandma Irene's ballerina?

Shit! His radio was in his basement office, along with everyone else's. They never kept them on during guest nights.

Shit, shit, shit!

Cal hauled his ass back down the grand stairs, ran to the main doors, and worked the heavy, ratcheting mechanism that scissored inch-wide steel tongues into matching sockets in the top and bottom of the jamb.

Didn't have to worry about the back doors, they

were shuttered with decorative-looking but highly functional security gates that would take a blowtorch or large truck to open without the key.

Service entrance also not a problem. Guests were absolutely not allowed anywhere near hot stoves. Certainly not after an evening of free champagne.

So. Back upstairs. Number Forty had to be somewhere, and he knew every stinkin' nook and cranny in this place. Even a few he'd managed to keep secret from the rest of the staff.

Maybe not from old Larry the Handyman, but...

Damn. Who the hell would take an old lady's most prized possession? From her own bedroom? There was stealing, and there was just plain *wrong*.

He crept now, or at least he tried to. His breathing might be a little heavy from running up and down the stairs, shopping walks or not.

He was definitely sweating inside the torture chamber of his period butler's garb.

Bedroom after sitting room, he checked every door not normally locked.

Nothing. Nothing. Noth...

At the end of the family wing, Kent the Smaller Super Cat lay on his belly, whiskers twitching left and right along the crack under the mawster suite's water closet door.

Which was shut.

Which was silly, because the 1875-era WC was *also* behind protective plexiglass, and certainly not available for guest use.

"Hello?" he called, striding down the hall. "Who's in there? I've called the sheriff's office, and—"

The door burst open, shoving Kent out of the way.

The cat fuzzed up twice his normal size—his Super Suit—and streaked in a very un-Super way back toward Grandma's bedroom.

A pile of magenta velvet topped with Professional Soccer Mom hair replaced Kent on the hallway carpet, heading full-tilt for the service stairs in overpriced white walking shoes.

"Hold it right there!" Cal yelled, hoping to stop her before she...

The woman screamed before she made it halfway down, the scream turning into a series of thumps and groans as she finished her downward journey in a clump of flailing arms and legs.

The oversized sequin purse hit the stairs long before its owner hit the industrial green and white tiles in the kitchen below. Fortunately for her, a couple of the kitcheneers had heard the commotion and managed to catch her before her hair dented the vinyl.

Beside the purse sat a crystal ball which had rolled free when PSM dropped the bag. Cal snatched it up, checking for any cracks or other damage. He tugged a tiny silver key from beneath his shirt, wound the ballerina just a little. Just to check.

As the tiny dancer gave a twirl and a spin, Clark the Super Chonk lay right where he'd been when the PSM with the Sticky Fingers had, once again, not been watching her feet.

Silly, wonderful, *Super* Cat, part of a Crime-Fighter Pair Extraordinaire.

"Thank you, buddy," Cal said, rubbing that massive head until Clark's eyes, as green as a certain superhero's bane, closed above a throat full of purr.

4

THE REST of the dinner was a smash. Guests raved about the house, drooled over the food, drank enough of the free champagne that Katy paid the sleigh drivers extra to make sure no one walked or drove back to their accommodations.

Cal managed to make it in for the last round of farewells as thirty-nine of the guests left through the unbarred main doors.

And as one of the guests left through the kitchen and the service entrance with wrists tucked securely behind her back, passing through a gauntlet of DAR reps, manor staff, and one family scion and his assistant director, all of whom had ritualistic Victorian discipline in their eyes.

She carried no ID in that oversized purse, which besides the ballerina also held several pieces of vintage silverware, an ivory faucet handle from the downstairs washroom, and a couple of Wentworth Manor ballpoints.

Maybe Magpie Molly could be the arch-nemesis of the Super Cats?

Sheriff Duncan, who didn't hold to the old-timey stuff nearly as much as the folks at Wentworth Manor, had come on the double, carrying a nifty little gadget that let him snag a couple of prints right there in the museum office and send them along for processing.

PSM—and Cal needed to stop calling her that, since the Professional Soccer Mom hair had come right off, revealing a head covered with short, bristly spikes—still wouldn't say anything, but the sheriff said a whole lot of museums and houses open for tours all through the area had reported items missing over the past few months.

Be hard to get matching prints at those places after all this time, but maybe they'd get lucky at the most recent sites.

Besides, everyone in the room nearly fainted when Cal explained that the narwhal ivory, fineness of the carving, and the incredibly intricate two-hundred-year-old Swiss clockwork meant the ballerina had last been appraised for the insurance at something well north of ten grand.

Not that north of twenty would buy Grandma Irene's piece of her beloved Selena from him. She'd given everything else to the DAR, but this one thing she'd given to *him*. Given to him and asked him to keep safe after she was gone.

So far, he'd kept it where he thought it belonged. In Grandma Irene's room. But now he figured he better find a better hidey-hole.

Maybe Katy could help with that.

Once everyone was out of the house at last, the kitcheneers cleaning up and loading up, and Jake and his actor pals off for their own night of festivities, Cal walked the downstairs circuit.

Hm. He knew she hadn't left.

He found her upstairs, in Grandma Irene's room. The ballerina was still down in Cal's office, locked up tight in the heavy cube of Wentworth Family Safe. Dang thing probably outweighed Clark the Super Chonk, and no one was getting his grandma's dancer out of there without Cal's help.

Katy sat on the dressing table's padded bench, staring up at the empty space on the mantle where the little ballerina should be dancing.

Her heart wasn't leaking out, but he thought he saw some of it behind her eyes, just waiting its chance.

"Hey, Katy. What's up?"

There wasn't enough room on the bench for two, so he hunkered nearby, arms resting on his knees.

"Oh, I was just sitting here thinking about what you told me. About Mrs. Wentworth and Ms. Holland."

She stopped talking. Apparently now it was his turn. He tried for wise and worldly.

"Uh. Yeah."

Shit.

Katy gave him a peek from the corner of one eye bluer than Etta James after a heavy night of Greek tragedy.

Kent chose that moment to creep up and shove his head under Cal's hand. He absently scratched the furry head, trying to draw something, anything, from his Super Cat.

"Say, uh, Katy? I know we're busy and all tomorrow with the cleanup and year-end books, but maybe...uh...maybe..."

A perfect ginger eyebrow slowly worked its way skyward above that blue eye, and the corner of her mouth that he could see twitched a little.

Shit.

"Maybe...I mean, the Cakes and Ale...you know...uh..."

And that was when his other Super Cat Clark

decided to headbutt Cal in the butt, knocking him off balance and forward.

Cal flung his hands out, and of *course* one of them just *had* to land right on Katy's knee!

"Goddammit, Clark, you useless piece of..."

"Why, Mr. Wentworth! How *very* forward of you, sir!"

And Cal lost the rest of his words as Katy's hand came down on top of his.

"And yes, Cal. I'd love to have lunch or dinner at the C&A with you tomorrow."

Well, hell.

Cal managed to get to his feet without too much embarrassment, and Katy allowed him the honor of helping a lady to hers.

She didn't let go of his hand as they walked out of Grandma Irene's and headed toward the grand staircase.

Cal looked back one last time, saw Clark and Kent, the Amazing Super Cats, perched on Grandma Irene's bed, where they *knew* they weren't allowed.

But he'd let it slide. Just this once.

As Katy got the lights with her free hand, Cal could have sworn he heard a distant tinkling melody filling the room behind him.

Where a tiny ballerina danced, joined by two fabulous ladies of a different time.

28

JASON A. ADAMS

The Healing Power of Atole

To everyone who cooks with love.
And everyone who loves good cooking.

1

Sorrow is the last bite of a truly fine apple fritter.

Manual Ortega sat licking sweet tartness from his fingers unashamedly at the chrome and scarlet Formica dinette he had chosen especially for unit #3 in *La Pista,* his beloved two-up, two-down dingbat apartment building across from the Nellis Air Force Base flight line, in a part of Las Vegas that could out-noise even the famous Strip when all jets were scrambled.

Bought two years ago with the retirement funds he'd stashed away during three decades of bachelor life fixing flyboy's girlfriends at the base across the road, the building had allowed him to scrounge the salvage shops and reproduction services until the place had been rescued from threadbare and seedy squalor to a near-perfect mid-century modern masterpiece, matched only by his beautiful 1959 Cadillac Coupe Deville, she of the emerald cheeks and mighty fins.

As Christmas approached, the drop in temperature and months of airing any room not occupied by a living creature requiring summertime AC, the repro wood paneling, linoleum, and other projects had hopefully gasped their last outgas, and could begin absorbing their proper aromas. A lady's perfume. The scents of good cooking. The glue he used to create the gossamer tissue-and-balsa clipper ships he liked to fly in the park on fine days.

Across the table, Trisha Macintyre sat beside her young man, Bill Jackson. Trisha was his second tenant, having arrived a few months after Bill.

Bill was a good kid. Early thirties. Computer guy who did computer things on night shift. Took the bus everywhere he went. Manny wasn't sure why that was, but a man's decisions are private, no? At least when they don't affect others.

If Bill was the young man whose privacy he respected—as much as the son of a Catholic and Latino herd could do—then Trisha, who'd moved in halfway through October, was the young lady he wished to sweep onto his white horse and pledge his loyalty to.

She'd come to them still learning to walk on a leg

of metal and plastic instead of flesh. From the rejection of a disgusting piece of filth who'd broken their engagement after her injury. All she had was a few boxes of necessaries and her beloved Janie the *buena chica.*

Every day Bill made the difficult journey from #2 to #3, no matter how terrible the weather.

In Las Vegas, except for summer heatstroke, the weather wasn't much of a deterrent over the three feet between their front doors.

Of course she and Bill had fallen together. How could they not? Bill had risked his life to save Trisha's doggie from rush hour traffic when the *buena chica* had pulled her leash from Trisha's hand and charged across the lanes. What more could he have done that that?

Manny was happy for them. Happy for them in a way he'd long ago decided wasn't in his own future.

Bill whispered something to Trisha, who clapped a hand to her mouth to cover the giggles as her tan face took on a much more rosy hue.

Under the table, Janie—Trisha's *buena chica* of a bully girl—thumped her tail, sneaking the very tip of her boxy nose up above the table's edge, pining and on the brink of a starvation that could only be cured through pastry.

"Oh, Manny. Something I meant to tell you,"

Trisha said, swatting the back of Bill's head. Good girl. Train him right.

"*Si*, pretty lady? What can an old man do for you?" He bowed slightly, squeezing his befrittered belly enough that a small belch escaped.

"Classy, Manny," Bill said, rolling his turquoise eyes. "Real classy." Then he let out his own belch, one with far more gusto than Manny's poor effort.

"It's not anything you can do for *me*," she said. And now young Trisha looked uncomfortable, her gaze fixed on her daisy-printed placemat. "It's just... well, my mother wants to come stay for a few days. Maybe until Christmas? Are guests okay for that many days?"

"Your mother is welcome to stay as long as she likes, of course," Manny said, surprised. "As long as *you* like. I have no problem, but why will she stay here? I thought she lived over in Summerlin."

A furious roar shattered the outside air, and without missing a beat Trisha and Bill grabbed anything that might try to walk off the table as a pair of F-15s punched their afterburners across the boulevard.

Janie was coming along. She put her head on Trisha's lap and whined, instead of yiking her way to the bedroom and her safety crate.

"She does, yeah. She says the bug people are

coming to spray for termites, and she's worried about the chemicals. My dad...I mean, she doesn't trust anything that might be toxic, no matter what the safety sheets say."

"Termites. Yes. One must crush those little *cabrones* at first chance." He rubbed his chin, looking around at Trisha's meager collection of furniture. Including the puffy blue mini-couch, and the full bed in the other room. Comfortable for one, cozy for two.

"Tell you what," he said, snapping his fingers. "I have a futon couch stored in #4. It's a bit on the firm side, but it's clean and I have linens to fit. Bill? Perhaps you could help an old man switch it out with our young Ms. Macintyre's loveseat?"

Trisha's whole body slacked down, and Manny thought he would get one of the kisses she reserved for Bill or Janie.

"Oh, that would be *wonderful*, Manny! Let me just check the cushions for any of Janie's things."

"Young Trisha, I loved my own parents dearly. But I would not have for long if I had to share a bed with either of them."

Ten minutes, two rawhide bones, and a huge rubber squeaky toy later, the futon he kept for his own visitors nestled under the apartment's living room window, a stack of neatly folded sheets the color of duty blues resting on one arm.

Bill's wrist beeped, and he stretched until his back popped loudly.

"That's me away to the salt mine. I better go grab that bus."

"Don't worry about the bus," Manny said. "I shall honor you with a ride upon my trusty stallion. Don't you feel the blessing of the Saints? Have a quiet and peaceful night, young lady. Come on, *gringo*."

2
___

THIS *LOOKED* like the right address.

Paula Macintyre sat in the apartment building's entry lot, starting up at the blinding white stucco and the space-age fifties lettering spelling out *La Pista* in glowing light the color of a streetwalker's lipstick.

She shook herself. Tish said this place was safe, and she was a grown woman. But Paula had never been comfortable on the east side of town.

She had no reason to feel that way, she knew. She worked with people of all colors and backgrounds in the counting room of Aladdin's Kasbah, the casino she'd been at longer than Tish had been alive.

But for all that, sometimes she was still that scared girl from the Appalachian hollers, following her man across the country to a place the preachers said was nothing but the Devil's playground.

Besides, Tish still seemed so…well, *fragile* wasn't the right word. Or was it? Crippled by a drunk, abandoned by an…an…

"*Asshole,*" she whispered under her breath, still sure her long-gone mother would tan her fanny for using such a word.

She saw the enormous green antique car Tish told her was the only one parked regularly, and eased into a space at the other end, uncomfortable at the thought of so much building above her.

The parking area looked clean, and the other car positively glowed with a light of its own. Paula was sure she could do her makeup in the reflection of that hood, which had to be the size of a king bed.

"Ah, you must be Mrs. Macintyre. I am very pleased to meet you, *mi amiga.*"

Paula controlled her startled flinch, and turned to see a squat man with the deeply tanned skin and black hair of strong Hispanic roots. A little silver glinted in his hair, which was cropped short and cut in that razor-edged way she usually only saw on servicemen.

"My name is Manual Ortega," he said, holding out one thick hand that could easily swallow both of hers. "And this is my humble tenement. May I take your bags and show you to young Trisha's door?"

He *seemed* friendly. His smile crinkled the corners of his eyes into soft wrinkles that she was sure had rarely held anger.

"Thank you," she said. "That's very kind of you."

She popped the trunk, went to take her weekend bag. It didn't hold much, but she could always run back to the house for fresh clothes.

"No, no. Please. Allow me. You are our guest, *si?*"

He reached past her and pulled the heavy bag from the trunk like a box of tissue paper, then waved toward a set of stairs climbing up through the middle of the building.

"Young Trisha is on the third floor, to the left."

"Third floor? I'm sorry, but do you have anything lower down? Her leg—"

"I assure you, Mrs. Macintyre. Señorita Trisha insisted on the top floor."

That was just like her. And she probably never let anyone help her with groceries or that dog of hers or anything else!

Stop it, Paula. You promised.

She had. But it was so, so hard to let her baby do for herself, when...

When.

She said nothing for the rest of the climb, her thoughts running around like a gerbil in one of those wire wheels. Racing and spinning, and not getting anywhere useful.

"Ah, here we are." The landlord knocked on a door with a spiky number 3. Three quick raps. Solid and sure.

"Just a minute!"

A minute passed. Then another.

Paula's heart thumped away.

"Mr. Ortega, she's taking quite a while. Do you think we should—"

The landlord patted her arm with his free hand.

"Don't worry, Mrs. Macintyre. I have heard Trisha call for help when she truly needs it, and she can shatter the sky better than the fighter planes across the way. Also, you must call me Manny. I insist. Mr. Ortega makes the Mexican food in the grocery store, yes?"

Was he making fun of her?

Well, no. He didn't seem to be. He had one of the calmest, most serene smiles she'd ever seen.

She envied him that. Yes, she did.

Then she heard the strange thump-step Tish had now. And the clicking of that dog of hers.

"She is doing quite well, Mrs. Macintyre," Mr. Ortega whispered as the footsteps stopped. "You can be very proud of her."

Before she could reply, the door opened.

"Hey, Ma. Glad you found it okay. Thanks for grabbing her bag, Manny."

Tish *looked* okay. She'd gained a little weight, but not too much. Her shorts revealed legs with good muscle, just like Dr. Hersch said she should have.

And she looked happy.

"Sorry for the wait, Ma," she said, scratching her dog's head. "I was...taking a personal moment in a private part of the apartment."

"I believe she was relieving herself," Manny whispered in a voice Paula was sure carried halfway down the street. She turned to him, meaning to dress him down for such a crude remark, but Tish caught her in a hug before she could get him.

"It's good to see you," she said. "I'm glad you decided to stay here instead of some hotel. Even if you could get a free room at work."

That horrible man chuckled as he walked in like he owned the place, setting Paula's bag by a foldout under the window.

At least Tish had curtains.

"Well, I didn't want to stay in the comp rooms. You know those floors are still smoking, and they reserve all the non-smoking for paying guests."

She looked around the tiny apartment. A miniature living room held the couch, a narrow coffee table *a la* IKEA, a couple of floor lamps that looked like something from an old scotch ad. And a flat-screen TV mounted to the wall like an invading time-traveler.

The floors were covered with the same harvest gold linoleum that graced her parents' old house back home. The kitchen held curvy green appliances that might have come straight out of a vintage Sears catalog, but looked new. Maybe from one of those reproduction places?

"I will leave you two lovely ladies to your visit, while I go do battle with my preparations for tonight's *Las Posadas*. Trisha, Mrs. Macintyre, please let me know if there is anything at all I can do for either of you."

The strange landlord actually *bowed* before rubbing that dog's ears and walking back outside, before Paula thought to ask what *posadas* was. Didn't it mean hotel or something?

Once the door shut behind him, Paula turned to Tish.

"How are you doing, honey? Really?" She started to touch Tish's shoulder, lost control of her hand, and let it flop back down. She'd lost so much of the easiness they used to share. She wanted to say she didn't know why, but of course she did. The accident, the breakup, the physical therapy, of course those things had changed Tish in ways she couldn't understand.

But she tried. Surely Tish knew that.

"I'm fine, Ma," Tish said, going to the kitchen and taking a couple of tumblers from an upper cabinet. She still limped, but not nearly so much as she had when she first got the prosthetic. "Janie and I walk every day, a little further every day. I can handle just about everything around here, and I've got Manny and Bill for when I can't. Want some tea?"

"Sure. Thanks. Where *is* Bill anyway? I was hoping to meet him." And make her own assessment, no matter how much Tish gushed. Look how good her instincts had been *last* time.

"He's in bed. I told you, he works overnights. He'll be over around..." She looked up at one of those creepy old cat clocks, its eyes spying on the room as its tail ticked out the time. "Six. We usually eat together before he heads off to work."

Paula hoped so badly this Bill was a good man. Her Tish deserved someone to be good to her.

"Well, I look forward to it, honey. Mind if I use your private part of the apartment for a personal moment?" For the first time in a long time, maybe because of how happy Tish looked, maybe because she could see the tension sneaking in around the corners of Tish's eyes like it always seemed to when they were together anymore, she added in a loud whisper, "I need to relieve myself."

The surprised belly laugh that erupted from Tish was one of the most welcome sounds Paula had ever heard.

3

Manny had just finished his cooking when he thought he heard a woman crying in the parking garage, the soft sounds coming up and in through his open window. The evening was cool, but he always let the air come in for a taste when he cooked.

Not Trisha, which didn't surprise him. That was one tough *chica*. So, who?

Turning off the gas and wiping his hands on a dishtowel, he took his heavy eight-cell flashlight from its hanger beside the door. Never knew when he might need light, and the thick aircraft aluminum trumped any skull around.

Once on the stairs heading down, he heard it more clearly. This was not hysterical sobbing, it was the gentle crying of sadness. Or of regret.

"Hello? Do you need any help?" he said as he got to the pavement.

He saw a woman sitting against a smart little Honda Civic, wearing jeans and a loose blouse that nearly matched the robin's egg paint.

It was Mrs. Macintyre.

She jerked when she saw him, dragging her palms over her eyes before wiping her nose with the back of her hand.

"I'm sorry, Mr. Ortega. I'm fine, really. I just..."

"Please, let me," he said, rushing to her and taking his hankie from his pocket. "Here, use this. I promise it works better than hands."

She gave him a watery laugh and took the cloth, wiping away her tears and smudging the dark streaks of mascara on her cheeks.

He thought he should do something. She was upset. But he didn't want to pry.

She blew her nose with a loud honk, started to hand the hankie back, then stared at it with horror.

"Oh my goodness! Your handkerchief. It's ruined, and it's all my fault!"

She buried her face in the soggy square as her shoulders shook some more.

Manny wasn't cut out for this. It's not like she was some airman he could slap on the back and put to work to keep his mind off things.

But, he'd just finished some of his grandmother's favorite sadness medicine.

He held out his hand. "Mrs. Macintyre, why don't you come with me. I have soap and water, which work far better than a hankie when the need is so great. I also have...what does your daughter say? Aid and succor in the form of sucrose."

He thought for a minute she'd stay right there on the dusty concrete, but she finally nodded, sniffled a mighty sniffle, and took his hand.

He hummed as they walked. Didn't ask her any questions. He didn't really know what questions to ask. *Are you upset?* seemed a little silly.

Back in his apartment, he sat her at his table and went to run hot water on a cloth and bring her a hand mirror. While she surveyed and repaired the damage, he went to the stove and dippered out a mug of steaming beverage.

"Here, madam," he said, setting the mug down beside her hand. "This is known to cure almost any ill that doesn't require surgery."

She smiled at him. A sad smile, but at least her eyes were dry. Red, but dry.

"Thank you, Mr. Ortega. I'm afraid I've made a mess of things with Tish. Again."

He nodded. Didn't say anything.

She took a sip from the mug, and her red eyes went wide.

"Oh my goodness, this is delicious! Like corn muffins in a glass! What is it?"

Manny felt his Cheerful Old Mexicano mask come on.

"That, my dear Mrs. Macintyre, is *atole*, a corn beverage sent down from the gods of ancient Mexico to heal wounded souls."

She watched him, took another, longer sip.

He shrugged. "It's Latino comfort food. Something sweet to fight off upset. It is also part of the traditional Las Posadas refreshment. I was about to take it to my auntie's house, since she's one of the Inns this year."

A line he recognized from young Trisha appeared between her eyes.

"I heard you say that before," she said. *"Las Posadas.* What is it?"

He refilled her mug, got one for himself, and sat down across from her.

"It is a tradition among Latinos. Goes way back a few hundred years. For the nine days before Christmas, the children 'help' Maria and José, Mary and Joseph, look for lodging at a different house in the barrio so she can rest and the Christ child can be born. Every night, they are turned away, although their rejection is followed by food, drink, and little gifts all around. The last night, the holy parents are finally allowed to stay, and all is right with the world."

The red was leaving her eyes. That was good. Her nose still had a little shine, but one repair at a time.

"That sounds nice," she said. "I'm sorry, am I keeping you? I can go if you need to. Go for a drive, maybe."

Manny was not at all good at this, but he believed in trying.

"What happened? Did you and Trisha have a quarrel?"

She sighed. Twisted the washcloth one way, then the other, her eyes on her hands.

"No," she finally said. "Not a quarrel, so much. It's just... I worry about her, and I fuss over her like a damn mother hen, whether I want to or not. But how can I not? She's my baby, and she's all alone for Christmas, and..."

She shook her head. Looked at Manny with eyes nearly the same color as his Caddy.

"Who am I kidding? *She's* not all alone for Christmas. *I* am."

She set the cloth on the table. Rolled it forward. Rolled it back. Manny waited, gave her time.

"My husband, Tish's father, passed away two years ago. Lung cancer. He never smoked, but thirty years working casino pits meant he might as well have been a carton-a-day man."

Manny nodded. That was one of many reasons he stayed away from the gaming houses.

"Anyway. I was alone for the first time in my life after that. For a few months, anyway. Then Tish was in the crash. Between losing her...losing her leg..." She swallowed. Gripped the edge of the table. "And then that son of a bitch threw her away like a broken lamp."

Somehow, Manny's hand had reached across the table and covered hers. He wasn't exactly sure when that happened, but he left it there. Wasn't that what you were supposed to do when someone needed sympathy?

"She came home to me. And I was able to do things for her she hadn't let me do when she was a teenager, let alone after she grew up. And I hate to say it. I enjoyed being able to coddle her. And that's what it was. Coddling. And worrying. I see how well she's doing. How happy she is. But I can't stop worrying, you know? And that makes me ask all the wrong questions and try to smother her and..."

She threw her hands up and laughed a not very happy laugh.

"I never had children of my own," he said, trying to pick through all the things he thought he should say. "But I come from a family a little larger than Mt. Everest. I did and do my share of helping with the raising." He patted her hand like an idiot. "It is okay to worry about her. That is *your* job as her mother. But she *is* going to push back. That is *her* job as your child, yes? She needs to be independent, especially if she feels you or others pity her because of her leg."

He'd seen that reaction many times. Among the Ortega clan, among airmen who suffered injury. That pride and stubbornness and self-pity that lashed out at those who only wanted to help.

"Tell you what," he said, rising to his feet. "If I don't get this atole to my auntie's house, then the Holy Virgin and her holy husband will give me holy hell. Would you do me the honor of joining me? We won't be gone more than a couple of hours, and that should give Trisha time to soothe her own guilt with Bill's help."

4

———

PAULA WASN'T sure how she ended up parked in a bright green Cadillac, watching a parade of children dressed in gold and silver costumes lead a donkey with a young woman on its back through the streets of what Mr. Ortega said was his *barrio*.

But she was glad she was here.

The parade was simply charming. She didn't understand the singing, but her companion told her what was going on at each step, and kept a mug filled with the creamy sweet a-tol-ay for her.

That alone was enough reason to cry in this man's arms as often as possible.

While they watched the parade, the rejection by a *very* old woman who must be Mr. Ortega's auntie, and the boisterous street party that followed, he told her of growing up here, of joining the Air Force to see the world, of coming back home when he finally retired when they forced him to.

He also told her how Tish made her way through her—albeit small—world with no patience or time for other people's pity. How Bill was completely head over heels for her, and had gotten his own nose nipped for trying to help too much.

His own nose nipped. What a fun way to put it, and she understood exactly what he meant. Her own nose was a little sore from earlier.

"So you must trust young Trisha. And young Bill," he said. "They are both very capable, and have each other for when capable is not enough."

"I do trust her," she said, feeling the traitorous moisture stinging her eyes. "And he seems like a wonderful young man. I just wish I knew some way I could tell her I'm sorry without telling her I'm sorry. To let her know it's not pity, it's just...just..."

"Just being her mama," he said. "I am no rocket scientist, but I have been known to put people at ease from time to time. If you'll trust me, I think I know a simple way you can reach out to her."

He explained his idea as they drove the few miles back to the apartment building.

And it *was* simple. So simple she'd never have thought of it, not in a million years.

They got back before nine. Manny—Mr. Ortega

—made her sit and wait while he came around the car to get her door. He was gentlemanly, that was for sure. And not hard to look at. And so *confident*. She wished she knew that little secret.

They walked up the stairs to the third floor, their hands only occasionally brushing together.

Bill opened the door when Mann—Mr. Ortega knocked. He really was a handsome young man, and the way he looked at Tish left no doubt in Paula's mind that he truly cared for her.

Tish was at the table. She didn't seem mad anymore, which was good. But she didn't quite meet Paula's eyes, either.

Mr. Ortega casually tapped her shoulder.

"I'm afraid I need to sit," he said, going to the pullout couch and flopping down. "I am filled to bursting with excellent food and far too much atole."

Tish's dog Janie came out of the bedroom and wagged her way to him, allowing him to rub her head until she grunted.

He caught her eye and winked.

Well, time to test his theory.

Paula went to sit beside him, lifted her arms in a stretch, and yawned.

"I'm beat," she said. "Say, Tish. Would you mind getting me a glass of tea?"

Tish stared at her.

"You want *me* to get *you* something?"

"If it's not too much trouble. Your poor old Ma's dogs are barking up a storm."

"Sure. Yeah. No problem."

Tish got up from the table, got the tea from the fridge and poured a glass. She brought it over to Paula, hardly limping at all. Probably no one who didn't know would even see it.

"Thanks, honey," Paula said, taking a drink. "Do you have anything planned for us tomorrow night? If not, Mr. Ortega's offered to take me to *Las Posadas* again."

Tish stared at her, open-mouthed. Bill looked at Mr. Ortega, one eyebrow reaching for the ceiling.

"A date?" Tish said, her smile turning into a rather impertinent grin. "Paula Lynn Macintyre, are you going on a *date*?"

"It is a religious observance," Mr. Ortega said. "One which I shall be attending alone, if your fair mother keeps refusing to call me Manny."

"You sly old bandito," Bill said. "And here I thought you were sworn to bachelorhood."

Paula's cheeks heated up, although she laughed along with everyone else.

It felt good to be in a room full of laughter. To see

Tish's fingers link through Bill's like it was the most natural thing in the world.

She didn't know if she was a threat to Manny's bachelorhood or not, but she was looking forward to a few more nights sitting in his car with him and watching the Las Posadas parades.

She jumped when something warm shoved up under her hand. Janie, asking impolitely for petting.

Well, why not? Tish liked Janie, and that was good enough for her.

Tish seemed to get along with Manny pretty well, come to think of it.

"Say, Manny," she said, putting her hand on his. "Do you think you could teach me how to make atole sometime?"

She tried not to see the smirk on Tish's face.

"My dear Paulita, I would be most happy to teach you anything at all, anytime you like."

Bill guffawed. Manny stared at him for a second, then turned a darker shade as he realized what he'd just said.

"I'm looking forward to it," Paula said, bold as brass.

More of that wonderful laughter filled the room, and overflowed Paula's heart.

Tish would be just fine.

And maybe. Just maybe…

She squeezed Manny's hand, glad when he squeezed back.

It was a start.

JASON A. ADAMS
Author of Sunlit Spirits and The Trouble With Vegans
If I'm Lyin'
I'm Dyin'

For Grampa, and all the other tellers of tales.

IF I'M LYIN' I'M DYIN'

I EVER TELL you 'bout the time I cotched me a ride with Santa Claus?

My name's Walt Colley, and I'm gonna tell you a story you might not believe, but if I'm lyin', I'm dyin'. Anyone who knows me knows I ain't one to tell tales, so if I'm telling it, you can take it to the bank.

Back in '74, this was. The coal mines was booming, and enough trees had growed back after them loggers shaved down all the lumber that the mountains was starting to look purty again. 'Specially when we got some of that good, wet December snow that stuck all in the branches and covered everything with 'niller frosting.

Yessir, Christmastime sure was a sight back in them days. We got snow most years plumb from Halloween on through to Easter. It'd come down right smart at night, paint everything white, and then mostly melt off by dinnertime next day. Except on the shady side of the ridge. Or on up in January or February when the mercury didn't bother comin' up outta the bulb.

The mud got awful cold when it snuck down in a man's boots, but mornings was still a purty sight.

I'd just got sacked from the Moss Three coal warshin' plant the very day before Christmas Eve. Avery Hicks—him that was foreman on the night shift back then, y'understand—Avery had snuck up on me on my break and caught me with a bottle. I done my work just fine, even better after a nip or two, but that churchin' do-gooder fired me right then and there.

So there I was. Awake in the wee hours of Christmas Eve. A body can't turn their clock around in just a day or two, and I was as wide-eyed as a hoot owl when midnight struck.

I'd decided to take me a walk in the woods, since the night's snow had started up right on time. A big ol' full moon lit up the backside of the clouds, and what with all the white in the trees and on the ground, it was like walking through a cheesecake.

Now maybe I'd had a nip or five, and maybe not. But what happened next is the ever-lovin' truth as I live and breathe. Hand to God, it is.

That nip I might or might not have had was from a batch I'd made myself. Pure corn, and more kick than a hoss that just got the gelding band. The trees were sorta moving around, and my eyeballs wanted to cross like a Catholic at mass. I figured it might be time to head on back home.

The dang trail kept wanting to get out from under my feet, but I was doing all right until it took a curve without telling me. My left foot came down and just kept on a-goin'. I'd gone and walked right off the side of the mountain!

I must have been higher up than I thought, because I just fell and fell, and kept right on falling. Not so bad, though. I felt plumb relaxed, and figured now was as good a time for a nap as any.

I'd just put my hands behind my head and crossed my feet, settled back into the air and right cozy, when I smacked down hard on something and got my wind knocked right out.

I laid there trying to suck in some air, and wondering what all the sharp corners digging into my back might be. On either side, the trees whipped past so fast they were only white, green, and brown blurs.

I got up on my elbows and looked around. I'd fetched up in the back of a great big stake-side truck. Bigger'n any coal hauler or tractor trailer I ever seen. The bed was full of boxes and bags, all wrapped up in red, green, and gold paper. Bright bows all over everything.

All along the bed, four to a side, a gaggle of little ladies in pointy red hats and green, fur-lined miniskirts were flinging the boxes out every time the truck passed over a house. Somehow, all the boxes went straight down the chimneys, or else squeezed in under the back door. Something to see, it was!

I just sat there admiring the view, especially whenever one of the dears bent over the bedrail for better aim, when the gal with the tallest, pointiest hat saw me. Tallest or not, she wasn't but a little thing, maybe four foot tall. Her ears looked kinda pointy under the hat, and she had some of the palest blonde hair I ever saw, almost as pale as all that leg coming down out of her skirt.

Well, she grabbed me by the arm, and a goodly grip she had, let me tell you. I had bruises all over the place for nigh on a week.

"You can't be back here!" she yelled at me. "This is a work area, no drunks allowed! You need to get in the cab and talk to the foreman!"

She drug me up to the front of the bed, and all but pushed me through the cab's back window. I went through head first and landed on the jouncy bench seat.

"Ho-Ho-Howdy there, Walt!"

I got myself turned rightways up, and took a gander at the trucker. He was a mighty big fella, all decked out in bright red coverhauls, with hands covered up in puffy black mittens on the truck's wheel. Between three feet of cotton wool on his chin, the red gimmie cap scrunched down on his head, and the spangly gold sunglasses covered with lightning bolts and TCBs, I couldn't hardly see any face at all.

The cab was a sight too, that's for sure. Twinkly red, green, and blue lights were strung all around the windshield and side glass. Holly branches chock full of red berries covered the dash. The twin cupholders held a steaming Stanley thermos on one side and a clump of candy canes in the other. Elvis banged out *Santa Bring My Baby Back* from the Philco. Out on the front of the truck's hood, I saw a little metal bull-dog, flashing red so bright it brought the water to my eyes.

"You been a mighty naughty boy this year, Walt."

I looked over and seen Santa giving me the hairy eyeball. He took the wheel with his knees and poured himself a cup from the thermos.

"What the hell you talkin' about, Santy?" I got to say, I was a mite peeved. "I ain't done nothin' wrong this year that I know of."

I *did* know of a few teeny little things, but surely all that hadn't got out and made news.

Santa took a spiral notepad from his chest pocket and flipped through the pages.

"Says right here you up and got yourself fired for lushin' on the job."

"That weren't my fault! Avery Hicks always had it in for me!"

Santa flipped back through the pad. "Says here your pay got docked in October when you ran a bucket loader into the slurry pond."

"Ground was muddy. Anybody coulda done that."

"Maybe not anybody with breath on their booze."

I always thought Santa was a jolly-type fella, but he was starting to get my back up.

"And how about back in May, when you didn't show for work and the boys came and found you passed out in your drawers out behind your woodshed?"

"A nip or two's just a good man's fault," I muttered. I felt the fire in my face and the truth in my gut, though.

"I'd say you got more faults than Californy, Walt," he said, dropping the notepad back in his pocket. "But, lucky for you it's Christmas and I've a mind to let you work things out and get back off the naughty list, what say?"

What else could I say? Didn't sound like much of a deal, but he was offering me the first break I'd had in a 'coon's age.

"Sounds good to me," I said. "You just let me know what needs doin' and I'll do 'er."

"In that case, you better grab a-hold of something. I'm about to put the hammer down." He slid the back window open again and yelled back over his shoulder. "Hey Connie, Dorie, Cutie, and Vickie! Strap down, we're runnin' slow and I got a schedule to keep!"

The women in back plunked down on the wheel wells and bungeed themselves to the cargo hooks right before Santa slap-shifted down to third and stomped the gas. Presents flew off the bed as he spun the wheel and yanked it down until the truck was headed straight up toward the sky.

"Hang on, Walt! Things is gonna get squirrely!" Santa was grinnin' and ho-ho-ho-ing fit to bust, and I figured we'd be all right.

We shot up through the clouds, which smeared the windows with sticky goop. I cranked mine down far enough so I could reach out and grab a handful. I smelled mighty sweet, so I tried me a taste. Them clouds were the best cotton candy I ever had, and still hold that record.

"Where we headed?" I shouted over all the

racket from the engine and from the gobs of sugar floss smackin' against the windshield.

"Right there, Walt," he said, pointing at the full moon. "We need to pick up a special delivery."

Wellsir, that moon kept on getting bigger and bigger, until it looked bigger than UT's football stadium. Santa aimed toward the Man's biggest freckle, and we touched down and skidded to a stop, the truck's big air brakes squallin' like a bobcat in heat.

"Time to earn some good graces," Santa said. "Come on down out the truck and get to work."

I clumb down and looked around. Up close like this, the moon looked just as green and purty as a Granny Smith fresh off the tree. Smelled different, though. Smelled like a pizza parlor right when they pull the pie out.

Santa handed me a bucket and a long-handled shovel.

"Noleta Campbell's feeling puny. She's been active in the Ladies' Auxiliary and Friends of the Library all year, so I figure she deserves her Christmas wish. Get to diggin', and fill that bucket up with green cheese so's she can have her favorite tuna melt."

So it really *was* made of green cheese. That's how I know all those moon landings was faked. Walt

Colley was the first man—or at least the first *human* man—to step foot on the moon, don't never let anyone tell you different.

I filled that bucket with green moon cheese lickety-split, then we loaded back up and headed back towards Earth. I spent a couple of hours helping the dears in back throw out the presents to all the houses. We tossed 'em down to cabins, four-square farm houses, big tall apartment buildings, castles, even a few igloos.

Finally, just about the time my back wanted to give out, the last present got chucked down toward a grass hut somewhere over the Pacific. I was plumb beat, and covered up with scratches and bruises from bumping around in the back of Santa's souped-up delivery truck.

I knocked on the back window and hollered in at Santa. "I reckon we're about done with everything! How's about dropping me back at the homeplace on your way by?"

Santa didn't say a word, just slid the window closed and hit the gas pedal a little harder.

I knew then that he meant to keep me on past my shift.

I turned around and saw the dears had pulled on side-striped brown trousers and jackets just like the deputies wear. They'd also got all those bungee cords they used for seatbelts, and were stretching them and looking plumb mean.

Now Momma Colley didn't raise no nitwits. I figured it might be time to punch out and head home.

I peeked over the side and saw we was over a snow-covered hillside and not too high up. I didn't think first, I just jumped over the rails and tried to keep my knees bent.

Well, I hit the ground hard and started rollin'. I don't know how many rocks and tree roots I bounced off of, but by the time I hit bottom, I'd had it. I got one good look at tail lights flashin' away up in the sky, then I checked out for a while.

When I come to, I was layin' in a bed in the Saint Mary's emergency ward. I had gauze and tape all over me, and felt banged up pretty good. But nothing was broke, and I could waggle all my fingers and toes, so I didn't complain much.

My luck was in, for sure. I'd jumped out right over the place where I'd been walking earlier that night, and they found me at the foot of the ridge. Doc said I was bluer'n cue chalk when they finally got me here, but I must've had enough antifreeze in my system to keep me going. He told me later that he'd writ a paper on my BAC and got it published in one of them doctor magazines.

I learned me a lesson that Christmas. After I got

out of the hospital, I cut back on the squeezin's. I don't take more than just a teensy small nip here and there anymore. I got me a decent job at the gravel quarry, and ain't wrecked a bucket loader in nigh on fifty years. I got to thank Santa for helping me that much. Fair's fair.

So that's the story of the night I got to ride with Santa Claus and why I know for sure he's just as real as anything.

It's all true, every word, and I've got the scars to prove it.

If I'm lyin', I'm dyin'.

JASON A. ADAMS

Author of Sunlit Spirits and The Trouble With Vegans

The Twelve Steps Of

Christmas

To everyone who keeps pushing the daisies down.

1

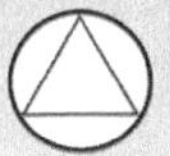

December snow is a lovely sight.

Today was the twenty-third. All up and down the parking lot and access road, cars frosted with white sat silent. Naked trees and still-green rhododendrons were outlined and capped with fluffy white. No cars came in or out, and hadn't all day judging from the smooth blanket covering the pavement.

Cardinals chipped and chirped as they chased one another from branch to branch, their scarlet coats bright against a perfect sky, bluer than Smokey's flashers and dotted with puffball clouds. The homey smell of wood smoke drifted from the old farmhouse across a bare stubbly field that waited patiently for next year's corn.

Chuck Cantrell stepped out on the porch of

Halfway Home, the place he'd been staying for the last couple of months. It had started life as a farmhouse, been cut up into boarding rooms for itinerant workers, and now served as the only halfway house for recovering alcoholics and addicts in three counties.

Chuck liked it here. He had some freedom, but also felt safe from himself. His seven housemates came and went, and were okay guys for the most part. In the two months he'd laid his weary head in room three, only one person had gotten himself kicked out for sneaking hootch in his room.

Standing on the whitewashed porch, in front of the whitewashed house with its black shutters, white foam cup of Swiss Miss in hand, Chuck felt ready to brave the day. He loved the cheap stuff, even if he had to drink it quick enough so's the cup wouldn't melt. He sipped carefully, trying not to burn his tongue again, slurping up one of those weird slimy plastic blobs that tried mightily to pass for marshmallows.

Fake marshmallows or not, the cloyingly sweet cocoa passing over lips and gums (look out abdomen, here she comes!) took him straight back to boyhood. Drinking gallons of the stuff while the Mormon Tabernacle Choir belted out dog-whistle pitched Christmas carols on the reel-to-reel player. Him, his folks, and his older brother would sit around on the scratchy, turd-colored burlap couch and armchair, footie-clad feet up on the world's heaviest mock-oak coffee table, and bicker about presents, ham, the correct way to drink cocoa and eggnog.

He missed those days, back when everyone got along and no one had restraining orders.

This Christmas was challenging, though.

Two months out of the rehab center and three months from his last bender, Chuck was finally starting to feel a tiny bit more stable. The ol' brain fog had gradually started to clear, and he could actually remember things. What he needed from the store, what appointments he had that week, where he'd left his phone and his keys.

He'd also started packing on a few muscles. A career spent designing computer networks hadn't exactly given him the body of a Greek god, and half a lifetime chasing the next drunk made him look more like a Laughing Buddha.

Since getting sober, though, he'd been working part time on a construction crew. He barely knew which end of a hammer to swing, so he mostly did the scut work. Hauling lumber, hauling bricks, hauling just about anything. He was a damn good hauler, turned out. The job left him worn out at the end of the day, and he slept early, long, and hard.

Didn't leave much time for thinking, and that was just fine. The inside of his head was a snarled up mess of emotions that he had to *deal* with now, dammit. His days of numbing it all down were hopefully behind him.

He'd be fine.

Today would be a good day, and he was doing fine.

Nothing was going to shake his cool today.

Positive thinking, positive outlook, positive actions.

The army surplus field jacket kept him warm enough, and the day wasn't so cold he had to try and navigate the world in mittens. Good toboggan one of the orderlies at the center liked to knit for all his recovs as he called them.

Warm, full of hot chocolate, good to go.

All well and good.

But this would be his first sober Christmas in… well, in a longish while. Not much worry about trouble with the family, not since the separation papers were all signed and official.

Chuck *maybe* fantasized a little about showing up unannounced and being welcomed home with group hugs all around.

Or *maybe* he could keep working at making sure his head stayed out of his ass and let Mary and the kids have the best day they could. They knew how to get in touch if they'd a mind. He'd mailed cards and a couple of small gifts, bought with his own earned cash.

No big sob stories, no pleading, no whining. Just a note to say he loved them and hoped they had a great Christmas.

Being an actual rational adult kinda felt good, and kinda sucked at the same time. Not that he had a whole lot of experience on how it *should* feel.

And he didn't have any time to mull it all over. A battered Chevy S-10 pickup truck with a giant eagle decal on the hood came pulling into the Halfway Home parking lot. It might have started out red, but was now mostly dust and scratch colored. With one last wheezy rattle and cough of blue smoke, it came to a stop.

The driver's door opened, and something between a grizzly bear and a small mountain squeezed out, wearing jeans and a black t-shirt that proclaimed in huge neon green letters, "Never Give Up!"

"Hey, Chuck. Ready, buddy?" The voice was surprisingly mild for such an enormous guy.

"Ready and willing, good sir," Chuck replied with a smile and a two-finger salute.

The bear-mountain was Fred S., Chuck's

sponsor and pretty much best friend. Fred topped six-three, and went maybe two-sixty on the scale. Tattoos all over bulging forearms and biceps, plus the ponytail that pulled all his hair backward until the top of his head could blind a guy in the right light made him look like someone you really didn't want to notice you on a dark street.

But Fred was sixteen years sober, and had taken Chuck under his wing at the treatment center, when Chuck was still confused and shaking like a leaf in a hurricane. The big man had one of the best hearts Chuck had ever run across.

Ex-Special Forces (he wouldn't say which), ex-gang banger, ex-drunk, ex-druggie, ex-you name it.

Now, Fred worked as a counselor at the treatment center, took shifts as house monitor at Halfway Home, and gave Chuck the rides he needed. He also helped Chuck figure out which thoughts made sense, and when he needed to reconsider some brilliant idea or other.

And he'd taken a chance on Chuck and put him to work on his construction crew. That was something Chuck still didn't understand and would never be able to repay.

Chuck climbed in the truck's passenger door, marveled as Fred somehow greased his way in behind the wheel.

Fred cranked up, gave a satisfied nod at the backfire, and headed out to the main road. This morning's meeting was at the Clubhouse, which didn't look like any clubhouse Chuck had ever seen. It was a storefront in a mostly-empty mini-mall out by Highway 7, about five miles from the Home.

Meetings ran every other hour, swapping out between AA and NA. Chuck sat in on a couple each day. He didn't care which, since he'd never met anyone in the rooms who wouldn't take whatever they could get when they were in a hurt.

They sat in companionable silence for a few minutes. Fred drove with one hand on the wheel and the other resting on the stickshift.

Chuck stared out the window at the clear blue sky with its cottonball clouds, the snow-covered fields, the houses and shops. He picked at his jeans, fingernails flicking at the seams.

"So how you doing, Chuck?" Fred asked, eyes still lazily watching the broken white lines slip past.

"Okay, I guess. I mean, I'm fine." The hand not worrying his jeans drummed on the door's armrest.

"Gimme a better answer, buddy. No copouts."

Damn. Fred didn't like one-word answers when it came to how Chuck was doing.

But he *was* okay.

Fine.

He just...just...

And it spilled out.

"I miss my wife, Fred. Her and the kids. I don't think I'll be seeing them for Christmas and that's eating at me. I want to call her, call *them*, but I don't want to upset the family any more than I already have, and I have no flippin' idea what to do about all of it."

"No shit." Fred glanced over at him and smiled. "Be crazy if you didn't feel that way. What'd ya have for breakfast?"

The sidetrack threw Chuck for a second, but he rallied. This wasn't the first time he had to deal with Fred's train of thought, which sometimes seemed more like a hovercraft than a train. A hovercraft in a high wind.

"Hot chocolate. Couple of cups. I wasn't really hung—"

A loud rumble from the vicinity of his navel outed the lie before he finished.

They both laughed. God, it felt good to laugh. Really laugh.

He'd missed that a lot the last few years.

"Tell ya what, buddy," Fred said, hitting his turn signal as he downshifted. "We'll skip the morning meeting and grab some eggs. My treat."

2

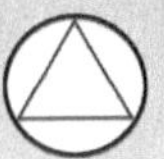

CHUCK SAT across from Fred at one of those somehow clean but greasy tables local hash-slinging joints always seemed to have. He told Fred stuff he hadn't even realized he'd been struggling with.

About how he wanted to spend Christmas with Mary and their girls, Sally and Joyce. Sal was heading toward thirteen, and Joyce had just turned ten. He'd already missed a big chunk of their childhoods, too blitzed to pay attention. He wanted to be in their lives, but was afraid they wouldn't ever want anything to do with him again.

He had no idea how to approach any of them, and it was weighing on him.

He hadn't even known all that was on his mind, at least not consciously. He'd been so busy making sure everything was *fine* and *okay* he forgot to check on the things that weren't.

Fred didn't say anything. Just sipped his coffee and nodded from time to time. When Chuck finally wound down, Fred set the mug down, folded his massive arms and leaned on the table, staring at him with that unblinking blue stare that always made Chuck feel peeled open.

Chuck waited.

Fred didn't say anything.

"So, that's about it, I guess," Chuck said. "Sounds stupid I know, but—"

"Shut up," Fred said, expression never changing. "So you feel like you blew it with your wife and kids, and you're having a hard time dealing with the idea of Christmas alone. That about right? A nice summary?"

"Uh, yeah, I guess."

Fred leaned back, grabbed his coffee mug, took a long drink.

"Sucks, don't it? You'll get through it, though. Just keep looking for the next right thing and doing it. Keep your feet on the ground and keep pushing the daisies down instead of up."

Chuck stared at his so-called sponsor.

"That's it, Fred? *That's* your advice? What the hell does that even mean, 'the next right thing'?"

"I dunno, buddy. We all have to look for our own right things. The simple version is TTBFN. Try to be fucking nice." Fred grinned at him again. "Hold doors open. Help little old ladies get stuff down off the top shelf. Don't leave the bathroom a friggin' mess."

"But what about Mary? And the kids?"

"What about them? You can't control that situation. Only thing you *can* control is how *you* act. I'm not giving you advice, but if it was me, I'd let things be on the family front for a little while. Don't tell them how much you've changed, let 'em see it for themselves. Things'll work out, they always do. But you have to be ready in case they don't work out the way you want. Now, let's eat and get our sorry asses to a meeting."

And that was all Fred would say on the subject.

Suddenly, Chuck was starving. His belly had apparently been full of nerves and bile, because once it was all out, he needed food like, well, like someone who hasn't eaten well for days.

Chuck raised a hand to signal the waitress. A hand that held not a trace of the DT boogie.

He plowed through a plate full of scrambled and toast, drank three cups of coffee, and polished off a side of cheese grits before he managed to push himself back. He'd know in a few minutes if the peach cobbler could squeeze in.

Fred drained the last of his umpteenth cup of coal, belched, and gave a quick shake of his head.

"Yeah, forgot to tell ya. The Clubhouse is getting fumigated this evening, so no meetings tomorrow while the crap settles out of the air. You been doing good, getting at least a couple a day, so you can take tomorrow and just chill at the Home. You'll still get your ninety in ninety, no sweat. So put your feet up on the coffee table. Watch bad TV. Take in a Hall-mark movie, maybe."

"You sure?" Chuck asked as Fred dropped bills on the table and they both stood and got their coats. "Need a hand with anything at the job site or anything?"

"Chuck, tomorrow's Christmas Eve. I ain't plan-ning on going anywhere *near* the job, and neither are you. I got some family stuff of my own to take care of. So try and relax a little, would ya? Part of this whole getting sober deal is learning how to do nothing when the time's right. Do nothing, and enjoy it."

3

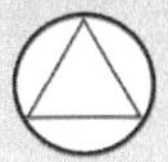

THEY GOT to the Clubhouse with half an hour to spare before the eleven o'clock. Chuck stood outside with the liar's club, telling stories and laughing some more. They were a great group, pretty even between men and women, but of all ages and social strata.

Jodie, a tall African-American with the shoulders of a boxer and a day job banging the gavel at some courthouse or other, had them rolling with a story about how he threatened to throw a cop in jail. While said cop was arresting him for drunk and disorderly.

Who but a group like this could guffaw over stories that involved so much dumbass thinking? Stories like Jodie's helped Chuck not feel so stupid when it came his time to share in the meeting.

No matter how boneheaded his stories were, someone had him beat.

Of course, they probably thought the same about him. Everyone's road to hell was different, and most people wouldn't trade mistakes.

Since starting this whole recovery jazz, Chuck felt like he truly fit in for the first time in his life.

They went inside, had a good old-fashioned gratitude meeting. Chuck talked about how he was grateful to be sober, grateful to Fred for giving him a chance to work, grateful he'd remember Christmas Day so long as he kept doing what he was doing.

He tried to feel good about the people who spoke of being grateful for the chance to spend the holidays with their families. He *was* happy for them.

But jealous as hell all the same.

The meeting closed out with the usual hand holding and Ah Faddah. Fred made the announcement about the Clubhouse closing at six that evening for the bug sprayers.

"What about Christmas Day?" asked a newcomer woman named Gina, a little nervously. "Will there be meetings on Christmas?"

"You bet," Fred said. "Doors will open at nine in the morning, and we'll keep the coffee on for the duration."

Several people breathed a sigh of relief.

As they left, Chuck looked at the lights decorating the Ace Hardware two doors down.

"Think there'll be much of a crowd on Christmas Day? Won't most people be home with their families?"

"You'd be surprised," Fred said as he unlocked the passenger door. "People need a place to go on holidays even more than other days. Sometimes *because* of their families. But you'll get to see for yourself. I'm gonna need you to open up and stick around until I can get here." He took a shiny brass key from his pocket and handed it to Chuck. "Think you can do that, buddy?"

Chuck stared at the key in his hand. Gulped.

Fred clapped him on the back with a paw the size of a hubcap. "Buck up, pal. All ya gotta do is open the doors and start the sludge pot. I won't even make ya chair any meetings. This time. Hop in, let's get you back to the Home. Don't forget, sock feet and bad TV all day tomorrow. Call me if ya need, don't matter what time."

4

———

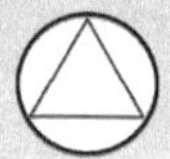

CHUCK SWEATED through his day of so-called indolence.

He tried. He really did.

Sock feet. Coffee table. The Hallmark Channel.

But his damn brain wouldn't leave him alone.

He was the only one in the Home today. Everyone else had Christmas Eve plans of one sort or another. He tried calling Fred, got voicemail. So he left a somewhat coherent message, and did the only thing he could think of that might get his mind off his mind.

By the time Fred called him back, Halfway Home sparkled from top to bottom. He'd washed windows, swept and mopped all the public floors, scrubbed the kitchen counters down to the bedrock.

His arms and back were threatening to go on strike when the phone finally rang.

"Hey, buddy. What's up?"

"Hey, Fred. Just needed to talk to somebody. I've been thinking again."

"Uh-oh. That's always trouble for guys like us."

Chuck heard laughter in the background.

"I don't want to keep you. Go ahead and get back to the family. I'm just doing a little cleaning around the place, and—"

"Don't worry about it. I got time. Talk to me, Chuck."

So he did. Not about anything important, just chatted. It felt good to just chat. Fred already knew what was eating at Chuck, no need to go over all that again.

By the time they said their goodbyes and hung up, he felt better.

Not perfect, not great, but better.

Maybe he'd give Hallmark another chance.

Huh. Turned out he liked several of the movies after all.

5

———————

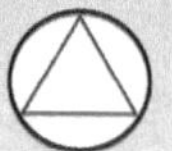

CHRISTMAS MORNING DAWNED bright and clear. The thermometer read right at thirty-two, not bad for December, and the weatherman promised a high close to forty.

Chuck decided he'd walk the five miles to the Clubhouse. If he kept up a good clip he'd stay plenty warm, and the walk would do him good.

He left the Home at seven, and hustled up the road. Hardly any cars were out, and he smiled and waved off the few who offered him a lift. It felt good to be out on the road by his lonesome.

Counting his steps kept the demons at bay, and he made it to eleven thousand four hundred and sixty-eight by the time he slotted the shiny brass key in the Clubhouse's glass door at eight-fifteen.

Gina came in just as the first pot of coffee

finished its noisy drip cycle, and helped him get the readings and pamphlets laid out on the long tables. They were joined by a dozen others by nine o'clock, and the first meeting of Christmas Day got underway.

Chuck was surprised by the soft camaraderie of the group. He'd never noticed before.

Before, he'd been New Guy, too busy worrying about not sounding stupid to pay much attention to everyone else. Things were different today.

Today, the Clubhouse was *his* responsibility.

He knew some of the folks who came in, got to know others. People glad to have a place to go on Christmas Day, glad to have others to share the day with.

Over the next few hours, he brewed dozens of pots of coffee, both hi-test and decaf. He chaired a couple of meetings, sat and listened at a couple more. People came and people went, but he didn't think he saw less than ten folks at any given time. Chuck shared his story, shot the shit between meetings, introduced himself time and time again.

It struck him around three when they sat down to several steaming pizzas, loudly blessing the local Dominos and tipping the delivery girl handsomely, that he was having a good day.

No, better than good.

Chuck felt great, actually. He was truly enjoying himself, and hadn't thought about Mary and the girls more than a couple of times all day.

Part of it was staying busy, of course, but part of it was the sense of belonging. Of helping out by helping others. Yeah, he wasn't changing the world or saving lives, but he was here, making sure the doors stayed open and the coffee stayed fresh.

He was sharing what little experience, strength, and hope he had, and got to soak some in from all the others.

The last slice of cheese pizza sat lonely in the last box, while a bunch of ex-drunks too polite to do more than stare greedily instead of dueling to the death tried to ignore it. The bell over the door chimed, and Chuck stood and turned, ready to welcome the latest addition to the day's festivities.

And stopped dead.

Mary came in, followed by Fred.

Chuck couldn't do more than try to winch his jaw back up. He wanted to say something. Anything. But there was some sort of major disconnect in his brain wiring right then.

"Hey buddy. Told ya I'd make it," Fred said, grinning like a cat in a canary-processing plant.

Chuck goggled his gaze between Fred and Mary. She looked so damn good in her poofy blue winter coat, the one with the fake fur hood. Her cheeks had that rosy blush she always got when the temperature went south of sixty. Her ebony curls had that tousled look they only got when she'd had her hood up.

"Hello Chuck," she said. She wasn't smiling, but she wasn't frowning either.

"H...Hi, Mary. How are you?" Eloquent as always, but at least he got some kind of words out.

"I'm fine. You look better."

Chuck choked on a laugh. God he wanted to take her in his arms.

Instead, he shoved his hands in his pockets. Gave her a smile.

"Yeah, well. That's a pretty low bar, considering." This time she laughed.

"How did you... What brings you out here, Mar? It's great to see you, but I wasn't expecting to."

"Blame Fred," she said. "He called me, told me I might want to come see how you're doing. We...we talked. Quite a bit."

Chuck shot a glare at Fred. "How the hell did you know Mary's number?"

Fred gave him that goddamn grin of his.

"Ya gotta quit leaving your phone laying around, buddy. Oh, and there's this great new feature phones have, where you can make it so you need a code to unlock it. You might want to look into that."

Chuck felt his eyes rolling. "What happed to rigorous honesty, oh sponsor-mine?"

"Hey, did I tell you I *didn't* sneak and check your contacts?"

He pondered the possibility of taking Fred out. Wondered what sorts of power tools would do the trick.

"We've been outside for a while, Chuck," Mary said. "I've been watching you. Watching how you've been taking care of people in here."

"Not really. I just make the coffee and straighten up in between meetings."

"No, you do more than that. You've been talking with people. And it looks like you've been listening, too. I think this suits you, and you certainly seem calmer and happier than I've seen you in a long, long time."

He didn't have an answer for that. Just looked at his feet. Kicked the carpet with one toe.

"Sally and Joyce miss you, you know."

"I..." He had to swallow. Swallow hard. "I miss them too, Mary. And I miss you. I'm really, really sorr—"

"Don't," she said, raising a hand. "Not right now, okay? I'm not making any promises, and I don't want you to either. But I think it would be good for the girls if you want to come by later on this evening and tell them Merry Christmas. They're at my mother's now, but maybe around seven? You can hang out for an hour or so. Yeah, an hour would be good, for now."

Chuck didn't know what to say. He looked at Fred, who only shrugged.

"Your call, buddy. I said you had to stay until I got here, and I'm here."

He looked back at Mary. Saw her looking back at him.

Not with welcoming desire, not by a long shot, but still.

She had just offered him a Christmas gift bigger than any he had a right to.

"I'd love that. Thank you. Thank you so much, Mary. Look, you go on back to your mom and the girls. I'll...I'll text you when I'm on the way."

She put her hand on his arm. Just for a second, then she drew back. Turned to leave.

"Call me when you're on the way, okay? I'll let the girls know you're coming."

Chuck's eyes burned as he watched her walk out to her little Corolla. Car could use a good wash and wax. Get the salt off.

Maybe she'd let him do that for her.

He felt Fred's heavy arm fall across his shoulders.

"Good woman there, buddy. Don't blow it. One hour's all you get today, but it's a start."

"Can...can you maybe give me a ride over?"

"Sure thing, buddy. Not a problem. And Chuck?"

"Yeah, Fred?"

"Merry Christmas, you old smoothie, you."

And Chuck felt more of that glorious, wonderful laughter bubble up and out.

JASON A. ADAMS
Author of Canine Cupid and Moulin Rouge
Convenience Store
Christmas

To all the family members we weren't born with.

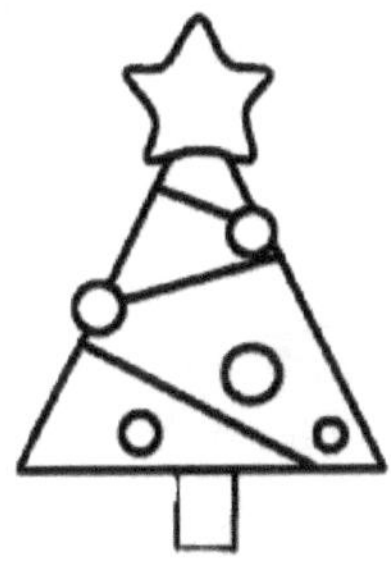

Oʜ, the traffic outside was frightful. But the tunes inside delightful.

Stuart Michaelson finished spraying faux snow across the base of the Stuart's Stop 'N Shop frontage glass walls, bringing it up the sides a little as he hummed along with The Waitresses and *Christmas Wrapping*. The spray-on variety was the only snow anyone in Atlanta was likely to see, unless a stray flake or two shut down the city some extra-cold night.

Up at the register, Susie sat with some gigantic book about long-dead people propped on the counter, sipping from an oversize mug full of hot cider so spiced that Stuart's eyes burned even at this distance. *Interesting* was the best way to describe how the aroma of her wassail went with the usual smells of strong coffee and hot dog that always filled the place.

Susie was one of his two helpers—his on-the-book helpers—and the one who'd been with him the longest. A perky nineteen-year-old, she studied dead people at the college up the way, and always seemed to be cramming for some test or other. This time, it was midyear finals. Last push before she headed home at the end of the week to somewhere in Tennessee to spend the holidays with her folks.

Five-five and mighty alive, Susie always put extra effort into clothing that showed how much she didn't care. For all her eye-rolling disdain for the world, her ponytail had changed from its usual pink to a more festive scarlet in keeping with the season. Good kid.

Mike, Stuart's other helper, had already left for his uncle's place in Tahoe.

Stuart himself would be right here with Bobby for the next three weeks, keeping the store open from six in the morning to eleven at night, Christmas Eve and Day included.

Not like he had any family left to gather with.

Not that he would've anyway. Family get-togethers were always trouble.

He had his store.

Bobby had his cat.

Behind Stuart, Bobby shuffled uneasily from foot

to foot, his sneakered feet coated in the dull silver of brand-new duct tape, the only thing holding his ancient kicks together. At least his brown corduroy pants and blue work shirt were relatively new. Stuart had bought them last month, dirtied them up a little in a park, and given them to his pal.

Bobby wouldn't let Stuart buy him clothes. But stuff Stuart "found?" That was okay.

"Please, Mr. Stuart—I mean Stuart—do you want me to wash all the white powder away, please?"

He'd brought Bobby in from the streets a few months ago, when the strange homeless man's cat Pete had broken his leg. He'd cut a deal with Bobby. Wash the windows, sweep the floors. Wash his hide from time to time in the standalone shower Stuart had installed in the stock room.

Do all that, and Bobby and Pete could stay as long as they needed to. Stuart did his best to pay Bobby, but the odd duck refused more than the occasional dollar bill or handful of coins. Stuart had finally convinced him he and Pete could browse the shelves for grub, as long as neither went overboard.

Ever since, Bobby and Pete lived behind the store, in a plywood shed Stuart had convinced the code inspectors was for extra supplies. He'd tried to get Bobby to crash at his place, but Bobby said he couldn't sleep indoors. Got too anxious. Felt trapped.

But he could handle the shed, which was enough like a dumpster.

Stuart did his best, and his best would have to do.

He was pretty sure Doreen, his most frequent health code snoop, knew the deal. But she also absolutely refused to look inside Bobby's castle.

She also never seemed to notice any paw prints on the sales counter, bless her.

"Nah, not this time, Bobby. You can wash the outside, for sure. But leave this side of the glass alone until I tell you, okay? It's part of the holiday decorations."

Stuart straightened up, leaning back with his hands on his spine until he felt the welcome pops run all the way from tail to hackles.

The convenience store which comprised the Michaelson Realm was always as spotless as Stuart and Bobby could keep it, but with the big December festivities on the way, they'd gone the extra mile.

Plastic candy canes big enough for Goliath's walking sticks hung from the ceiling, along with dreidels the size of cash registers. Strings of lights in Kwanzaa greens and reds blinked around the edges of the ceiling and along the tops of stock cabinets, reflecting up from the mirror-polished speckled white tiles on the floor.

Stuart wasn't much for holiday hoo-hah, but

plenty of customers were. Besides, it was nice to have the occasional change to the day-in, day-out.

The entrance doors whooshed open, letting in an arctic blast that might have dipped into the fifties.

"Hey, young Bobby! How you do?"

Stuart didn't need to see the puff of white hair or the mahogany face under the red feathered chapeaux. That voice, full of pure Old Atlanta, said it all.

Bobby muttered something more or less polite, and shuffled toward the stockroom door. He still hadn't gotten the hang of people, outside of Stuart and Susie, who'd been none too pleased when Bobby joined them, but had since sort of taken the older man under her much younger wing and was now his de facto big sister.

"Hey there, Miz Annabelle. How are you this fine day?" Stuart said, dropping his empty snow can in the trash and wiping his hands on his pocket rag. "Out hunting your Christmas goose?"

Through the glass, he could see her whale of a car, a Lincoln Continental at least forty years old and at least as brightly waxed as the Stop 'N Shop's floors. And wondered yet again how she managed to drive the thing. The old dear couldn't possibly see over the steering wheel.

"Goose? Now why would I cook goose when my

two grandbabies, those that have Fat Bubba's Barbecue, already got the grill full of good hardwood and a gret big ol' chunk of cow ready to roast?" She laughed, showing a set of dazzling white, and most likely store-bought teeth. "You and young Bobby ought to come down and fix a plate on the day. That boy needs to get some meat on him."

Stuart laughed along and carried Miz Annabelle's purchases to the counter so Susie could ring the old gal up. The usual salt and vinegar chips, a diet co-cola, and a *National Enquirer* (got to keep an eye on all them rascals).

Susie took Miz Annabelle's money and starting putting things in a plastic bag. She felt the chips, frowned, and held up a finger.

"Mr. Michaelson? These feel all crunched up. Maybe you should get Miss A a different bag."

"Ain't a thing wrong with—" Miss Annabelle started, but that finger with its black-polished nail jutted even more fiercely.

"Okay, okay," Stuart said, holding up his hands in surrender. "Sit tight, Miz Annabelle."

He went to get another bag of acid chips. He saw Bobby peeking around the stockroom door, and a much smaller gray face closer to the floor. Pete best not sneak out while customers were in the store.

He found what he judged to be acceptable potato

chips, and turned back toward the register. He saw Susie leaned way over the counter while Miz Annabelle nodded, those LED teeth flashing in a broad grin that took about thirty years off her seamed face.

Now what was all that about?

"Here you go," he said, putting the new chips in the bag. "What are you two plotting and scheming?"

"Don't worry about it, Mr. Michaelson," Susie said, turning back to her tome. *Advance of the Visigoths in the Western Roman Empire,* this one was. Stuart got a headache just reading the title.

"Lady business," Miz Annabelle said, patting his arm. "Don't you fret none, young man."

2

"Mrow?"

A gray-furred body leapt up beside the cash register and shoved its head under Stuart's hand.

"Dammit, Pete. You know you can't be in here," Stuart muttered, scratching as Pete turned his head this way and that, making sure the dumb human got all the right spots.

He was watching the front while Susie took a break from the books to restock the soda cooler. Bobby worked around her, plying his squeegee along the cooler doors until the glass turned plumb invisible.

Odd duck or not, the man sure could clean windows. And floors. Damn shame Stuart hadn't been able to prize anything about his family or history out of him. Poor guy would be stuck spending Christmas at the store with Stuart.

Susie came back up front as Bobby traded his squeegee for the Nixon-era rotary buffer and got to work polishing a floor already smoother than Teflon. As soon as the ancient machine started up, Pete hissed and made a break for the stockroom, scooting a stack of lottery blanks backward to the floor as he peeled out.

"You about ready to head for the hills?" Stuart asked. For once, Susie didn't have a book resting on the counter. Exams must be over. Day after tomorrow, he'd be on his own. Except for Bobby.

"Yeah, just about," she said, flipping her red ponytail over her shoulder. "In fact, if you have any errands you need to run for the store, you might want to do them today while I can cover. I *might* be here tomorrow, but maybe I'll have to leave a day early. Something might come up, you know?"

"Probably not a bad plan, Suze." Yeah, he could stand to pick up a bucket of floor polish. Maybe some more window cleaner, a case of coffee filters...

Heck. Be good to stock up on all the consumables, just in case things got crazy while his helpers were away.

"Too bad you can't get a tree for Bobby."

Stuart stopped staring at the list behind his eyes.

"Huh? A tree?"

"Sure." Susie smiled as Bobby worked the floor buffer like a born pro. "Maybe not a huge tree, but something you could put some lights on, and maybe a star on top. Who knows if Bobby's ever had a real Christmas tree?"

Stuart rubbed his chin, thinking.

"Well, why not? Wouldn't fit in his shed, but maybe in the back..."

Ponytail flew as Susie shook her head.

"No way, boss. My folks have cats. Tillie and Weasel. Every year the pops puts up a silly huge tree, covers it with ornaments, and then cusses a blue streak all the way through New Years because of how the cats climb up in the tree and knock all the ornaments off. All that stuff is just toys to them."

"Hm."

Stuart thought about Bobby, spending Christmas in his simple shed with only Pete for company.

"You know what, Suze? An errand run sounds like a fine idea. Things are pretty slow today. You good to cover for a few hours? Might be a little longer, but I'll call if I don't think I'll be back before seven or so. You can keep an eye on Bobby. Make sure he doesn't polish all the tile down to the dirt."

"Sure, Mr. Michaelson. Maybe I'll order in a pizza."

"You do that," he said, dropping a couple of twenties on the counter and paying more attention to his plans than her. "Go ahead and give the delivery driver a good tip. And save me a slice."

STUART GOT BACK to the store at a quarter to seven, patting himself on the back for making good time.

He'd been to every discount pet shop in a five mile radius, and the back of his truck was loaded down with bags.

A stop at the mall had taken a little longer, given the distance he'd had to park from the entrance this close to the Big Day, but he'd found a spot near his *other* stop, so that had all worked out.

He parked near the doors, made sure the tarp covered everything in the bed of the truck, and went inside, smiling as *Jack Frost and the Hooded Crow* greeted him.

Whatever she was learning up at the college, Stuart had taken it on himself to teach Susie about Jethro Tull.

And Susie was alone. Had Bobby gone out back, or disappeared on one of his occasional walkabouts?

"Hey, Mr. Michaelson, Get everything you need?"

Susie's feet were propped on an upturned milk crate as she leafed through the latest tattoo magazine. She looked somehow even more bored and disdainful of life in general than usual.

Stuart's hackles stood at attention. What was she up to?

"Yeah, I did. Where's Bobby at? And why is your smugmometer on high?"

"No idea what you're talking about, boss man. Bobby might be back in the stockroom. Maybe. How would *I* know?" She smiled lazily. Flipped another page in her magazine. Crossed her feet the other way.

Stuart's eyes narrowed. Nothing good could come of an attitude like that.

Before he could do...something...the stockroom door opened and Bobby came toward the counter at, if not a run, at least a fast shuffle, trailing tails of duct tape from his sneakers.

"Please Mr. Stuart, it wasn't me or Pete, I promise, please!"

Bobby looked cleaner than usual, his face pink with fresh scrubbing and flushed with red.

"Whoa now, Bobby. What wasn't you?" He turned to squint at Susie some more. "*What* wasn't him, Susan Marie Gardener?"

"Ooo," she said, the smug little smuggle. "All three names! I must be in real trouble, huh, Papa?"

"I can always find a new employee, you know."

She smirked. "Another employee who'd let you run off to waste a whole day while she sat here and helped you make rent?"

Bobby tugged at his sleeve. "Please, Mr.—I mean Stuart. Pete and me didn't do anything in the back."

Stuart looked from Bobby's worried face to Susie's grin. He really should send both of them packing, dammit.

Finally, he threw up his hands. "Come on and show me what you didn't do, Bobby." He stopped at the front door to switch off the red neon *OPEN* sign and throw the deadbolt. Then he jabbed his own finger at his soon-to-be-ex-employee. "And *you* come right along with us, missy."

"Sure thing, boss man. Be glad to."

Susie stood up, stretched a big stretch, and sauntered back toward the stockroom, straightening that bright red ponytail that really wasn't professional at all.

Bobby shuffled along behind Stuart, hands wringing over and over.

And it had started out as such a good day.

Susie turned to face him and Bobby, leaning against the wall beside the door, hands in the pockets of her ripped jeans.

"Well?" Stuart said. "Are you going to...what *is* that?"

Stuart smelled something coming from behind the stockroom door. Something that filled his mouth with water.

"I didn't do it!" Bobby whined behind him.

Susie put a black-nailed hand on the doorknob and pushed the door open.

"Why don't you see for yourself, Mr. Michaelson?"

Stuart's jaw headed for his shoes.

The stockroom was gone.

All the boxes and crates of dry goods had been pushed against the walls, leaving the center of the floor, a space nearly as large as the store out front, empty.

Except for a couple of couches, and a long table loaded down with food.

A puff of white hair under a pointy elf hat instead of her usual red marked Miz Annabelle as she went from one tray of ribs to another of roast beef to one that held bratwursts far superior to anything that had ever graced Stuart's rolling warmers out front.

Behind her, two enormous men, at least six-four, who looked so much alike they had to be twins, from gleaming shaved heads to biceps bigger than his leg moved along doing exactly what she told them. Elephants obeying a mouse.

At one end of the open space sat an electric fireplace shaped like a certain famous space villain's helmet, glowing with faux flames. On a rug in front lay a gray pile of laziness, next to a pile of shredded cow that looked to have started out much larger.

"Merry whatever you celebrate, Mr. Michaelson," Susie said, "And you too, Bobby."

She hugged them one after another, while the savvy business owner and street-smart survivor tried to dredge up anything useful to say.

Stuart's eyes smarted, from the sterno under the serving trays, probably. He blinked away the sting as Miz Annabelle came over with her own hugs.

"Merry Christmas, young man," she said, smacking a lipstick rose on his cheek. "You and young Bobby got no call to miss Christmas dinner, you just gonna get it a little bit early."

"Yeah," Susie said. "I know you both. You'll sit in this store all day, every day until me and Mike come back. So you're just gonna have to sit down and have Christmas with us. Or Hanukah, or whatever."

Stuart blinked faster. And felt his mouth widen as a frog tried to fill his throat.

"Susie...Miz Annabelle...I..."

"You *nothing*," Miz Annabelle said, patting his arm. "You go sit. Then you're gonna eat. My grand-babies make the best damn barbecue between here and Timbuktu."

He turned to his friend. "What say, Bobby? Will you stay and have some supper with us?"

Bobby stared at the ground as his duct-taped feet shuffled, but Stuart thought he saw a smile.

"Can Pete stay too, please?" Almost a whisper, but not a refusal to stay inside with people.

"You bet," Susie said, taking Bobby's hand and leading him to a chair. "Come on, Mr. Michaelson."

"Not just yet." Stuart wiped a hand across his eyes. "Miz Annabelle? You reckon one of your grand-babies could help me bring a few things in from my truck?"

The old woman paused from adding another pound of food to a plate tested to its limits. "'Course they will. Jeremy, you go on now and fetch what young Stuart tells you."

"Yes'm," said one of the two interchangeable giants. "You show me what, then show me where."

Another wide grin added to the grins already filling the room. "Then we gonna eat until you cry, Mr. Michaelson."

Ten minutes later, the Christmas tree Stuart had bought for Bobby and Pete stood beside the electric fire, covered with the hundred or more cat toys he'd picked up to stand in for traditional ornaments.

Bobby sat between Susie and Stuart, all three of them with a plate full of more barbecue, corn, mashed potatoes, and greens than any four humans could manage. They ate, trying not to choke with laughter whenever another cat toy came flying off the tree, revealing a pair of wide green eyes in the shadows behind.

Miz Annabelle and her grandbabies stayed and ate dinner with the Stop 'N Shop family and kept all the plates full until Stuart begged for mercy.

Susie blushed—actually *blushed* as red as her dyed ponytail—when Jeremy's brother Jonah said her spiced cider would make an angel beg for more.

Midnight was in its grave by the time all the trays were packed back into the twins' van, leftovers shared out or stored in the store's cooler, and foam cups filled with cider for Miz Annabelle and her grandbabies to take home.

Stuart waved after Jeremy and Jonah as they

drove away, and walked Miz Annabelle to her green tank of a car.

"I don't know how to thank you, ma'am," he said. "I sure do appreciate—"

"Hush now," she said, patting his arm. "You march right back in yonder and thank that young girl in there. Was her told me you and Bobby ain't got no people. Me and mine feel blessed we could share a little with y'all."

Stuart tried, but all he could do was nod and wave as she got in her car and drove away.

He walked back through the store, brushing his fingernails over the crystal-clear glass-fronts.

He hoped the Roman coin set got to Susie's parents' house in time. Not high-quality coins, but they sure were old.

Bobby would just have to swallow his pride and accept the new sneakers waiting for him under the tree.

Susie met him at the stockroom door, finger to her lips.

"Come here and check it out, Mr. Michaelson," she whispered, taking his hand and pointing at the couch nearest the still-glowing electric fire.

Bobby lay curled up on his side, Pete riding his shoulder.

Both of them were sound asleep.

Stuart pulled Susie from the room, softly shut the door.

"You heading back home tomorrow?" he said as they walked toward the exit. "Better get back to your place and grab some sleep yourself. Bad time of year to be driving tired."

"Yes, Papa," she said, rolling her eyes. "Don't worry, I won't get myself killed and leave you without your minion."

Then she surprised him with a huge bear hug.

"Merry Christmas, Mr. Michaelson. And tell Bobby for me, okay? And make sure he and Pete get enough to eat? I'll be back on the thirtieth to help out with New Years, I promise."

And then she was gone.

Damn good kid.

Stuart stared across the empty parking lot, then went back inside the empty store.

And didn't feel the least bit alone.

He went behind the counter and flipped on the store's music box, starting on the day's paperwork and whistling along while The Waitresses did their song about how a solo Christmas turned out to be not so solo in the end.

JASON A. ADAMS
LONG MAY IT RING

For the Santa Train and its crew. Long may it roll.

1

Boy, ain't the lights pretty?

I love this time of year, that stretch between Thanksgiving and Christmas, when the sleepy little town of Standifur goes hog wild with the decorating. Why, they got life-size and bigger Santa Clauses on just about every corner, all of 'em lit up on the inside and glowing like willy-wisps. Big ol' glass balls (they're really fiberglass, but let's leave that) in more colors than a sack of jellybeans hang from the street-lights and power poles, along with snowflakes a yard across and covered with those teeny fairy lights, looking like targets in a science-fiction shooting gallery.

All that plus I don't know how many miles of garland, tinsel, and ribbon swooping up and down over all the shop windows and doors all up and down

Main Street. Makes the whole town look like the best present under the best tree you ever saw.

And the smells! Lord God Amighty, all the gingerbread and pie and cookies and everything else to spike the ol' blood sugar covers the whole town with the purtiest stink you ever got up your sniffer. Fanny's Cupcakes serves up a dozen flavors with enough frosting that every endocrinologist in six counties faints. Able Charlie's Bakery runs through yeast like chickenpox through an elementary school, and nobody has to go without the best honey bread or apple stack cake in the whole world.

Now for me, there's another smell that trumps all that goodness, hands down. It's the furry, loamy, sulfury odor that drifts across the town when the Daughters of Standifur fire up the coal in the Standifur Christmas Forge in the middle of the traffic ring where Main and Maple cross.

That forge, it sure is something else. Like something out of an old movie about older times. Four feet high, made of river rock mudded together. As long as a tall man's arms tip to tip, and wide enough that two regular-sized fellers would have to stretch a fair bit to shake hands across the fire pot.

Beside the forge stand two things. One's a big ol' oak-trunk pole, one that's got a post-vise bolted to one side, the kind that's on a long pegleg to take the force of hammer or sledge. Opposite the vise hangs the biggest hand-crank blower I've ever seen. Bigger than a Champeen 400, with three different gear screws and a handle more than a yard long.

On the other side of the forge, sunk over two feet deep, sits a red oak stump that holds up a double-horned anvil the size of my first VW Bugaboo. Three hundred pounds if it's an ounce, and blacker than the Devil's worst sin.

Except for the top. That stretch of hardened steel looks big as an aircraft carrier's landing strip, and shines as bright as Arthur's sword.

When the Ds o' S get the coal burning and the blower blowing, I swear you can feel the heat plumb across town. The fire in that cast-iron belly glows so bright you'd swear the roundabout birthed its own star, and the sparks light up the night like all of summer's lightning bugs.

As to why there's a forge in the middle of town? And why it's the Daughters who're the ones cookin' coal into coke? And why it only gets fired up for the week before the Big Birthday every year?

Now *that's* a story.

THIS IS what I heard from Pap when I was still reading books with cardboard pages.

Pap, that's my granddaddy Jeremiah Isaac Mullins the Original (I'm number three, but call me Jerry), heard it from his own daddy, Silas, who wasn't more than a young'un himself when all this happened.

It started way on back in the year right after the boys won the first big foolishness over in Germany. Back then, Standifur was called Beehive, on account of the shape of all the coke and charcoal ovens that ran full tilt from sunup to sunup, cooking all the gunk out of the coal and wood sucked out or shaved off of the Appalachian ridges. Made some of the finest metallurgical fuel to be had, but all the stuff that come out of the smokestacks settled on porches and in lungs until you couldn't hear yourself think for all the hacking and choking.

I've seen plenty of pictures from that time, and all the buildings look the same. Anything wood was as gray as a granny's hair, and all the brick and stone black as pitch.

There's some as still say those were good years. Everybody had work if they wanted it, either down in the mines or up with the timbering crews. Everybody from bent old men down to boys who wouldn't need a shave for years to come.

Me? I'm glad those days are gone. Ever since they moved in the broadband and we got us a law school and pharmacy college, more folks are able to live off their brains and not by putting their spines on the line.

But that's just my opinion, and it ain't getting the story told any faster. Never mind.

Christmas back then wasn't quite the hullabaloo it is now. There wasn't any electric back then, for the WPA's dams and generators were still a dozen years down the line. Travel was rough for anyone who couldn't afford the train, and it might take a full day to go the twenty miles down the mountain to any bigger towns.

For all that everyone had paid work, the pay wasn't what you could call extravagant, and most folks lived hand to mouth. About the only places to buy were the Stanley General Store for household stuff, and the farm supply for anything needed outside the front door.

Folks sometimes ordered from the Sears & Roebuck when they had coins better than company scrip, but mostly the good people of Beehive made do with what they could grow or craft. That was fine most of the year, but come Christmas time, they wanted something they could wrap and put by the fireplace or coal stove for the kiddies.

The bosses who owned the mines and lumbering operations might have been as tight as a flea's bunghole, but they also had a streak of shrewd. And, I have to admit, there might have been a scruple or two lurking around the sumps of their hearts. At any rate, a few years before, they'd started up a new tradition.

The Santa Train.

This was a big to-do back then, and still is today. Every year, a bit before Christmas rolls around, the good people of the Franklin Railroad get Old Rudolph out from its shed at the Pikeville rail yard.

Old Rudolph is a hell of a beauty. She's an old Class M steamer, one of those they call Virginia Creepers for the way they could creep up the steep and twisty rail lines to every tucked-away coal or timber camp in the mountains.

Old Rudolph, draped all over with twinkly lights and tinsel, a red filter over her main lamp for that proper nose, pulls three classic First Class passenger cars, all green trim, velvet curtains, and glowing crystal chandeliers. These are loaded down with volunteers all dressed as elves with big gold "Santa's Helper" badges on their chests.

On the back porch of the bright red caboose, there's a great big platform, all done up with white porch posts and rail, with a huge puff of cotton batting on top for the snow.

And there stands the big man himself. Santa Claus. It's been Fred Piper wearing the suit my whole life, and I believe it would take dynamite to knock him out of the job. The Santa Train's been running close on a hundred years, and there's only been four Santas that whole time. As much as the train means to the common folk, it means just as much to those who ride it through.

At every old depot stop between Pikeville, Kentucky, and Kingsport, Tennessee, the train stops for a bit. The elves fling out toys, school supplies, wrapping paper, and decorations to the crowds that come in from all over. Some of 'em follow the train all the way down, but most are decent enough to only grab once.

See, the Santa Train, then and now, has one main

job. To make sure every tyke gets at least one present under the tree, and every house has at least some little something to dress the place up for the holiday.

I've seen tears on faces young and old every single year. And I'd imagine the same's been true for all the time the train's been running. Hasn't missed a trip in all those years, either.

Except once.

3

BACK WHEN THE town was still called Beehive, and my Great-Granddaddy Silas Mullins was still whiskerless, the year was winding down toward the Big Day.

Snow came and went in town and the valleys, but the ridges all wore their white winter caps that wouldn't melt off until April, probably. Cardinals chipped and chirped, flying around in their red coats like little harbingers of Santa himself, and squirrels jumped through the naked branches of those trees lucky enough to have ducked saw and axe, all fat and sassy from the nuts they'd, you know, squirreled away all through the year.

In town, a steady stream of ladies and bachelors wandered through the general store, snatching up every bit of flour, sugar, and molasses, all in a hurry to get back to their ovens and the latest batch of goodness.

Everybody was talking about their plans for Saturday, when the Santa Train would roll through town, giving out toys and candy and good cheer to all and sundry.

In the back of the store, a giant bear of a man hauled sacks from the grist mill's delivery wagon to the storeroom, piling up bags of flour, grits, and fine corn meal. The rear door was close to seven feet tall, and wide enough the wagon could almost park inside, but the sack tosser just about filled it up.

This was Bull Standifur. He was closer to seven feet than six, and half as wide across the shoulders. He never talked mean to anyone, but never much smiled either. He wasn't sour, just didn't ever wear his feelings out in the open.

His blue denim overalls had bands of different colors here and there where he'd had to open 'em up, even though they were the biggest size old man Stanley could order. The chest and shoulders of his longhandles looked like they'd been stuffed full of bowling balls, at least what you could see through the black tangle of hair and beard that ran halfway from hat to hip.

A regular Goliath was Bull Standifur.

He'd grown up son of one of the last full-time

blacksmiths in the county, and still did a bit of hammering for folks who farmed with older tools they couldn't get replacement parts for, but blacksmiths had gone the way of the dodo in most parts. He kept his hand in, but made his milk and bread hauling what needed hauling.

For all his size and wild hair, people sometimes didn't know Bull was in a room. He stepped as quiet as a mouse in his size eighteen work boots, and might not say more than a dozen words in the course of a day. He wasn't simple, not by a long sight. Bull was just quiet. Kept himself to himself.

That might be why no one realized he'd stopped bringing in the flour and meal when the ruckus kicked up.

Avery Phillips, the mail carrier all the way through the Truman years, came riding up the street, flogging his poor horse half to death and kicking up dust enough to rival the smoke from the coke ovens.

He ran into the general store, which was the closest thing Beehive had to a gathering hall, weeping like a child as he told the news.

Mountain slide. Big'un. Up toward Nasbie town. Most of Big Pilot Mountain had gone tumbling down into the river. Took out Grady Crossing, the hundred-foot-high, half-mile-long trestle that carried the rails into this part of the mountains.

Railroad said it might be six weeks before the line was reopened.

A squall went up from everyone in the store. Everyone but Bull Standifur.

No rails meant no trains.

No Santa Train.

No dollies for the little'uns. No toy ponies. No stuffed bears or kites or wind-up cars.

No Christmas, save for pies and cakes.

Well, there didn't seem much to do, except maybe try to carve wooden horses or make cornshuck dolls.

The folks who heard the news, and that would be everyone in walking distance by the time the sun went down that evening, all wiped their tears, gritted their teeth, and set about the grim chore of trying to make do without the cheery whistle of the Santa Train.

No one noticed Bull Standifur leave the general store with his empty wagon, heading not back toward the mill at all.

Heading instead for his homeplace.

And the forge and tools his daddy had passed down.

4

OVER THE NEXT WEEK, people in the general store started to talk. A few at first, standing around the pot-bellied stove that kept the chill from the pickle barrel, then more and more.

Soon everyone that wasn't at work in the mine or the kitchen filled old man Stanley's store from open to close, all of them with only one thing to talk about.

The roar of the fire coming from Bull Standifur's smithy house. The thunder and clang of hammer on iron.

Some of the womenfolk went to him after he'd thrown a horseshoe at the sheriff for interrupting. Tried to talk to him, or get him to talk to them. But all they got for their trouble was a bellow like the bull he took his nickname from. A cry for all the coal they could gather.

That wasn't like Bull at all. Not that silent giant who wouldn't say boo to a mouse.

And still the hammer fell, over and over.

So the ladies brought him his coal. They had to. The men of the town wouldn't come out and say as much, but the women knew. The boys were all scared to death that Bull had run crazy.

Janie Macintyre, a handsome woman who marmed three generations before she quit the schoolhouse, thought different. She'd known Bull since the century turned, and might have been the only one who remembered before he went quiet.

She allowed as how Bull was just *focused*. Focused on *what*, she'd not say.

But she thought maybe she knew.

5

———

It was Janie that got the ladies of the town organized. Got them working in shifts to bring sacks of coal in wagons or tied over the backs of mules and horses to feed the voracious furnace hidden behind the locked doors of Bull's smithy.

And it was the ladies who brought food and drink for the big man, for surely he needed as much stoking as his forge to keep his own fires hot.

Didn't take long for them to realize he wouldn't take normal food. No pork chops or mustard greens. No fried poke or bean fritters.

But he *would* take the gingerbread. And the cookies. And as much spiced eggnog as they could make.

People in town shook their heads. Poor Bull. Always such a good freight man and quiet soul. Done

143

lost his marbles. And now his house and barn were about to fall down, and his haul wagon was ready for the scrap pile.

Everything at the Standifur homeplace, *everything* made of steel or iron, down to the rims on his wagonwheels and the nails in the walls, had gone to the fire.

Janie let them talk, hiding her smile behind her hand.

She also passed word around, and soon husbands, fathers, and brothers started noticing things gone missing. Things like old bits of broken tools. Cast off cast iron. Wrought iron porch rails.

Any spare bit of metal, in fact.

And in Bull's smithy, the hammer came down like Zeus's thunderbolts loaded into a tommygun.

WHEN CHRISTMAS EVE FINALLY DAWNED, folks all up and down the hollers and ridges surrounding Beehive came out into the street or onto their porches.

Something was different that morning, and it took a bit to realize what it was.

The relentless hammering from Bull's smithy had stopped.

People gathered together in Stanley's store, flapping their jaws and trying to decide what to do.

Maybe he's out of coal at last, some said.

Might be he fell asleep, others opined.

None of the menfolk offered to go see. They all had those giant shoulders and arms in their minds. Dealing with the crazy was bad enough, but a madman the size of a full-grown hickory tree?

Finally Janie shushed up the crowd. *She'd* go check on Bull.

The men nodded. Good idea, they all said.

The ladies, all grim as old Death, nodded as well. They all had a feeling, but didn't want to put words to it.

Janie walked out of Beehive and up the path to the Standifur home place.

No smoke rose from house nor smithy.

In the trees around the house, not a squirrel nor bird made any sound.

Save for one lonely *chip* from a bright red cardinal, high up in a naked maple.

She tried to peep through the windows of the smithy, but they were all coated thick with soot and ash, and might as well have been tar paper for all she could see.

Next, she tried the plank door. It rolled open easily on its tracks, and a bright beam of sun lit up the inside.

Janie forgot how to breathe for a minute.

There stood the river-rock forge, cold and still.

There stood the blower and the vise.

And there stood the mighty double-horned anvil on its stump, its face shining bright as a brand-new dime, polished to a mirror by the endless days of hammer and red-hot iron.

Beside the tools of his undoing lay Bull Standifur, still in his long leather smith's apron, burned black by the heat of the fire, his five-pound crosspeen hammer and long hand-forged tongs crossed over his chest.

The sleeves and chest of his longhandle shirt were torn to ribbons, burst by the flexing of those massive muscles.

His broad-brimmed leather hat was drawn down over his face, and Janie thought for just a moment that he'd fallen asleep.

Across the crown and brim, scarlet feathers and deep-green holly leaves lay scattered.

She raised the hat, and almost didn't recognize Bull.

All his wild tangle of hair and beard was gone save for what his hat had covered. Singed away by the forge's heat.

A smile was on his face. Maybe the sweetest, gentlest smile Janie had ever seen. Certainly the first she'd ever seen on Bull.

But Bull's huge chest neither rose nor fell.

Janie dropped her chin and sent up a word to the Man on High for Bull's safe passage Home.

When she'd finished with that, she looked around the smithy, and instead of forgetting how to breathe, she gasped in wonder.

Every surface, every workbench and shelf and upturned crate, held the fruits of Bull's labor.

Tiny wrought iron horses with movable legs and manes of fine steel wire. Little doll babies with cunning smiles chiseled into their metal faces. Steel soldiers in a dozen poses. Toy steam shovels with working buckets and clever jointed tracks. Delicate flowers so fine they looked like blue-gray silk instead of the leftover scrap metal that birthed them.

Dozens upon dozens of toys. Hundreds. All forged from the bits and pieces she and the other ladies had brought up here by the powerful hands and even more powerful heart of the man laid out at her feet.

The Santa Train might not come that year, but no child for miles around would go without a Christmas present.

Janie bowed her head again, and liquid drops of her gratitude splashed down as she offered up all the thankful joy in her heart.

WELL, do I need to tell you that everyone who could walk, ride, or be carried showed up when Bull Standifur was sent off? The crowd was so big they had to scatter designated shouters all through to pass along the preacher's eulogy.

Bull was laid to rest in the clothes he'd been found in, apron and hat and all, his tools still crossed over his chest.

Right after the service, even before the jugs were passed to toast Bull on his way, all the adults of Beehive gathered at Stanley's general store for a vote. A vote that passed with nary a squeak of protest.

And later that day, the sign at the road coming into town was changed. Down came Beehive, and up went Standifur.

Bull's forge was hauled down stone by stone, each one numbered and marked out in a sketchbook so it could be put back together just so right there in the middle of Main and Maple. So too the anvil, blower, and vise.

And from that year to this, the Santa Train rolls through.

This year, old Fred Piper will stand at the back of the caboose, and he and the elves will fling goodies at folks all down the route.

Here in Standifur, Bull's forge will glow and the blower will blow, throwing sparks up at the sky until Christmas Eve dawns.

As soon as the sun peeks over the ridge that morning, young Lisa Powers, Janie's great-great-granddaughter, will stand beside the forge. She'll raise a cross-peen blacksmith's hammer on high, and bring it down one time on that mirror-bright anvil.

And the ring it makes will sing through the town, reminding all those who need reminding of how one year, a bull of a man with a heart bigger than a mountain saved Christmas.

Saved it with strength and fire and the last of his breath.

No one descended down from the good people of our corner of the mountains will ever forget Bull

Standifur, or what he taught us with his hammer and his spirit.

May the hammer ever fall and the anvil ever ring.

JASON A. ADAMS
Breakin' Up Christmas

Here's to the music makers.

1

___

Appalachian winter hung over Red Oak Ridge, turning Richard Tolliver's two-day trip to see his grandparents for Christmas one last time into what was looking more and more like some snow-blanketed, banjo-fired version of *Lost*.

Richard sat in Granny Earnestine's "good sittin' room," the one with the blood-red linoleum and wallpaper. Stared down at by dozens of disapproving black and white Tollivers and Colleys of yore, their beady eyes as bright as marbles following him everywhere he went while an ancient grandfather clock clacked away the seconds.

Even when he left the room, felt like.

He pulled his ancient Waltham pocket watch, one of many in his collection, from his pocket and checked it against the clock, pulling the knob and turning it until the tiny minute hand matched the larger one in the great wooden tower.

Granny Earnie had given him the silver 1921 watch as a trophy when he'd gotten tenure at the university, teaching Appalachian Culture Studies. She said it came from her Uncle Tommy, a local boy who'd run off after the first world war to join the merchant marines so he could stay out of the coal mines.

He loved Granny Earnie, and if he ever busted his gut scarfing down her buttermilk chicken and dumplings, they'd bury him with a smile on his face. But her good sittin' room gave him the ever-loving creeps. Had for twenty-six years, ever since he'd first been allowed to sit on the coarse, scratchy highback sofa.

The one with blood-red upholstery, naturally.

The mouth-watering aroma of those chicken and dumplings clashed with the sour sickroom reek emanating from the hospital bed under all those old pictures.

Richard's grandfather lay in that bed. His Pap.

What was left of him, anyway.

Walt Tolliver had always been a steel spring of a man, wiry and tough as nails. Never much bigger around than a broom handle, he'd still always amazed

Richard with the strength in his ropy arms, even past his seventieth birthday.

Now those arms looked like sticks draped with damp white rags. Pap's eyes hid halfway behind their lids, seeing who knew what through a morphine fog. The old man's gentle smile had given way to a slack hole that dribbled at the corners.

Richard had come when Granny Earnie called. His folks had already been and gone, along with the aunts, uncles, and cousins. All of them living close enough by to go home for the night, leaving Richard to stay with Granny and Pap, sleeping in the bedroom that had once been his dad's before heading back to the airport in the morning.

So of course a foot of snow had decided to fall overnight.

Granny puttered back and forth between the kitchen and the sitting room, bringing a blue stoneware bowl of dumplings for Richard, and a stainless-steel bowl of warm water for Pap. The hospice nurse wouldn't be in today. Or tomorrow. Not unless the weather turned a heck of a lot warmer and melted away some of the snow and ice.

Richard pushed his dumplings around with a spoon while Granny adjusted the oxygen tube under Pap's nostrils, then he decided to take his bowl back to the kitchen when Granny pulled the sheet back and started giving the skin-wrapped skeleton underneath a washdown.

"Bring...my fiddle..."

Richard stopped by the head of the bed at the low, raspy whisper. He didn't want to, but leaned down anyway, trying to close his nose to the stink of urine and vinegar and cancer breath.

Pap looked at him. Toward him, anyway. His eyes as bright and glittery as those in the rows of dead faces hanging on the walls.

"You say something, Pap?"

"I seen..." Coughs wracked his skeletal husk, bringing up bloody gobs of slime that Granny wiped away with her damp rag, crooning wordlessly as water ran down her cheeks.

"I...seen Santy Claus...break up Christmas..."

"That's good, Pap." Richard patted the bony hand wringing at the bedsheet. Then he scuttled into the kitchen, trying to blink his hot eyes into some kind of shape.

He wondered if hoping someone died soon could ever be forgiven.

2

———

RICHARD JERKED at the sound of water sloshing down the drain, his elbows slipping off Granny's pineboard table.

Granny Earnie stood at the sink, emptying out the wash bowl. Wringing out the rag she'd used to bathe Pap as best she could.

Richard watched her. Saw the set look on her face. The look that said she'd do what needed doing, no matter how she might feel about things.

The set look that was spoiled a little by the puffy redness around her eyes. He'd only known Pap for his own thirty-one years. She'd know him for nearly three quarters of a century.

"Granny? Does Pap have a fiddle? What was he asking for?"

She turned on the hot water to fill the bowl, adding a splash of bleach.

"Lord, honey. He ain't had a fiddle since back when we was just startin' to spark," she said in that high lonesome accent hardly anyone heard anymore. "I can't recollect exactly what happened, but I believe it got stole or some such. The old fool's just talkin' out his hind end."

Her voice broke a little, and she attacked the counter with her washrag, scrubbing phantom dirt away.

Richard's memory wandered back while Granny did her washing up. Pap humming while he worked on some torn-down piece of farm equipment. Singing hoary old ballads about love and murder. Clapping his gnarled, work-roughened hands and stamping his big thick-soled boots while Richard tried his best to clog like Granny showed him while she hammered on a dulcimer.

But he'd never seen *Pap* actually play an instrument.

Maybe he could slither down the icy road as far as town, see if Matt Blevins had the music store open. Matt had his own bluegrass band that played all the local festivals. He also supplied band students, and should have a student violin or something.

That might make a great going-away present for Pap.

Old Christmas, the local name for Epiphany on January 6, was only a couple of days away. One of those unique Appalachian holidays that still lurked in the corners of ridge and hollow. The old folks were dying out, taking a lot of their traditions with them, but enough still rattled around that Richard always saw a spark or two of recognition in his classes when he mentioned Old Christmas or wetting the baby or other leftovers from the old days.

"Hey, Granny? Need anything from town?"

3

THIS WAS PROBABLY A MISTAKE.

Richard half-walked, half-skated down Granny and Pap's winding road, grateful for the stout walking stick Pap kept by the door. Grateful for the heavy flannel-lined coat and pants. And for the bright afternoon sun and lack of clouds. The clouds that dumped all the snow last night had blown away, and the sky was as blue and brilliant as a Maharaja's sapphires.

The blacktop was almost a quarter of a mile from the house, and the gravel drive dropped nearly three hundred feet in that length. Several switchbacks allowed cars to make it up and down in all but the worst weather.

Unless a wet snow turned to ice.

He hadn't even considered trying his Buick. The

car was pretty sure-footed, but today was not the day to test it.

He eased around another curve, planting the walking stick firmly at each step, feeling for any slippage.

And wishing some saintly road crew had installed guard rails.

Leafless oak and poplar trees rose on either side. He felt no comfort realizing that he could look straight across at the canopy of hundred-foot-tall giants growing up from the frozen creek far below.

If he made the paved county road, he'd be fine. The town of Hibbett's Gap was only a mile or so away, and surely the plows and salt trucks had cleared the pavement by now.

Another step. Another poke at the snow-covered ice with the walking stick.

Finally! There was the blessed black streak of State Route 72 about fifty feet below him. Richard had never been so glad to see asphalt in his life.

Only a couple of hundred more yards.

Something rustled in the woods off to his right, and Richard had just enough time to see three brown streaks, one topped with at least ten points of antler, before the small group of deer exploded from the trees and ran straight toward him.

"Shit!" Then as first his walking stick slipped, then his feet, "*Double* shit!"

He stagger-stepped and waved his arms, the walking stick flying as he desperately pinwheeled.

Too close! Too close to the slippery, icy edge...

Richard grabbed for a tree trunk. A branch. Anything at all.

No good. He was over the side and rolling down the steep hillside toward the icy creek at the bottom of the narrow valley.

He tucked his arms in, knowing that trying to grab anything at this point might mean a broken arm.

He shouldn't have worried about his arms.

His head connected with something far harder than snow, and pain exploded inside his skull.

Was that a rock or a tree or...

4

"HEY. HEY THERE, YOUNG FELLER!"

Stop it. My brains are sloshing around.

"His eyes is workin', any road. He'p me, Stub. Let's us try and get him on his pins."

Something tugged at Richard's arms. Yanking him up from this comfortable bed.

"Huzzz..."

"Easy on, boy. Your head done dented enough rocks, I reckon."

Red spots filled the blackness, swirling around almost as bad as his belly, as cruel and uncaring hands hoisted him upright. With an effort, he got his eyes open.

"There now. You ain't dead yet, are ye?"

Through the speckles and spots, Richard saw two men dressed in blue button-up shirts under thick coats and denim pants held up with broad red suspenders. The one on the left, the one who still had him under the arms as he rocked and rolled, stood a few inches shy of Richard's five-ten, and had a lean, stringy build. Not skinny and underfed, just one of those human whippets built of wire and rawhide.

The older man standing to his right and a bit behind him was taller and broader, probably six-three. Huge biceps and forearms that put Popeye's to shame bulged the coarse brown sleeves of his coat. Richard wondered why the little guy had gotten body-hoisting duty.

"What d'ye think, Stub?" the one holding Richard said. "He simple, or just addled?"

"I'm...okay, I think," Richard said, shaking his head to clear it. Running his fingers gingerly over his scalp, he felt what promised to be a hell of a goose egg rising over his left ear. "Just bumped my head on the way down."

"He's all right," Stub yelled upward. Richard looked up at the road, and saw a couple more men, plus a couple of women looking down at them over the drop-off. The men were all dressed in a similar fashion to his two rescuers. The women wore long heavy dresses, heavy boots, and thick coats.

"Well thank the good Lord for that," one of the

women said. She looked young, maybe still a teenager.

"Y'all able to get back up here, or will I fetch some rope?" The second woman, maybe in her thirties, maybe forty-ish, had her hands on her hips and looked all business.

"Can ye climb, boy?" asked the younger man. "I'm Walt, by the by. Walt Tolliver. This here's Tommy Colley, but we all call him Stub on account of he's so dang puny."

They both held out their right hands, and Richard shook first one, then the other.

"Richard," he said. "Richard To...wait, did you say *Walt Tolliver?*" Right height, and with a gentle smile that looked all too familiar.

"We met before, Richard? You sound like away to me."

"No...that is, I don't think so. I...I used to know a Walter Tolliver back home. In...uh...Cincinnati."

Now the one called Stub looked at the one called Walt, who shrugged and grinned.

"I suppose there might be more'n one of me in the world. Whatcha think, Stub? I'm too dang purty to be one of a kind, ain't I?"

"Too big a dang fool, you mean," yelled the businessy woman. "Y'all haul that poor thing up here and let's get him doctored 'fore he dies of your stupid!"

The whole group laughed at that, and Richard let Stub and Walt help him pick his way up the hill, pulling their way from one tree to the next.

Tommy Colley. Tommy and Walt. Walt and Tommy.

Just how hard had he hit his head?

By the sun, he hadn't been out long. Maybe fifteen minutes. Damn lucky this group had come along. It wasn't cold enough to freeze yet, but if he'd laid there overnight...

And how had they seen him, anyway? Surely the bottom of the hollow wasn't visible from a car.

They made it over the lip to the road, and something in Richard's gut lurched sideways.

Instead of limestone gravel, the road was just two muddy ruts with a strip of winter-dry stubble in the middle.

A wagon drawn by a horse with overly long ears sat waiting. Was that a *mule*?

"You sure you're still with us?" Business lady asked. "You look awfully peaky. Here, best you take a swaller."

She reached into the back of the wagon and produced a heavy square bottle stoppered with a cork. Something tan and slightly oily looking sloshed inside. She pulled the cork, wiped the mouth of the bottle with her sleeve, and held it out to him.

"Go on, now. This here is some of Daddy's best applejack. If it don't knock the chill clean out of you, I'll eat Stub."

Richard took the bottle and took a cautious sip. His tongue caught fire and then went numb, the fire moving to his throat and down to his stomach before shooting right up and out the top of his head.

He coughed, took a bigger drink, and coughed again. The fire died away, leaving only a spreading warmth that he felt most strongly in his cheeks and watering eyes.

"Thank you, miss..."

"I'm Sadie Colley," she said, taking the bottle and recorking it. "And this little bit is Sarey. We're glad to know ye, Richard. Who's your people? And where's home?"

What the hell was going on here? Sadie was his great-grandmother's name, but who was Sarey? Or was it Sarah?

"I'm a Townshend," Richard said, pulling the last name of The Who's guitarist out of his butt. "My family is mostly in Ohio. I'm just traveling through. Got family in Boun County."

Stub—Uncle Tommy?—looked up at the sky.

"You ain't gonna make the depot in time for the last train. You best come along with us." The two women climbed up on the wagon's bench, the one called Sarey taking the mule's reins. "Get on up in back, Richard. You can't be walking without we see how bad your head is."

What the hell? He was probably in la-la land, but might as well enjoy the show. He let Stub and Walt help him up in the wagon's bed, and they joined him there. He saw the wagon held a couple of banjos, an autoharp, a dulcimer, and a battered fiddle tucked down in a crate filled with cloth.

"Where are we going?" he said. "Got some music planned?"

"Why, we're breakin' up Christmas, of course," Walt said. "Tonight's at my folks' place. We did Stub's last night."

"Breaking up Christmas? What's that?" Some distant tingle sputtered in Richard's memory. Maybe something he'd read in a Foxfire book?

"You mean y'all don't break up Christmas up yonder in Ohio?" Sarah said. She clapped her hands under her chin, her eyes going as wide as her smile. "Why, we break up Christmas every night between Christmas Day and Old Christmas. There's singin' and dancin' and all kinds of good things to eat and..." she peeked at Walt, who peeked right back. "And you'll see."

Now Sadie and Stub were looking back and forth

between Walt and Sarah. Stub looked grim, but Sadie only sighed and shook her head.

"Sarah Earnestine Colley," she said, and Richard gave the younger woman a doubletake so sharp he was sure he'd feel it in his neck later. "You will stay indoors where I can see you until time to go. You hear me, girl?"

Stub just garrumphed and folded those massive arms over his chest.

Walt grinned and blushed and reached out to twang a fiddle string.

5

TEN MINUTES OR SO LATER, the wagon pulled to a stop alongside several others in front of a small log house that was both familiar and not.

The walls were squared logs, and a couple of rooms were missing. But this was Pap's and Granny Earnie's house, all right. The white aluminum siding was a few decades down the road, and the extra bedrooms on the back weren't built yet. But the wide porch was there. So was the hen yard, although this was the first time Richard had seen hens in it since he'd been a wee lad.

This was definitely the mother of all weird dreams.

An old man had come out on the porch as Sadie drove the wagon into the yard. An older man Richard recognized from the faces of the dead on Granny Earnie's sitting-room wall.

"Who's y'friend?" asked the great-grandfather Richard had never met.

"Found him layin' half dead in the crick a piece down the way," Stub said. "Says his name's Townshend. Richard Townshend from up Cincinnati way, travelin' through to his people in Boun County."

"You make sure he ain't got no badge or a nose for whiskey?" his great-grandmother Abigail said, eyes narrowed.

"He took him a drink," Walt said, shrugging. That seemed enough to make him bona fide, and no one said any more about it as he helped carry the instruments into a house filled with people.

Walt and Stub introduced him around. He met more Tollivers and Colleys he knew as far older people, the ones still alive in his own time, anyway. He also met Standifurs, Holbrooks, Mullinses, Stanleys, and Blevinses.

All surnames he knew well.

Talk was lively and full of laughter. Even more so as bottles and earthenware jugs started going around.

The sky was darkening and folks were lighting kerosene lanterns when Stub picked up one of the banjos and struck a chord. The crowd went silent, then first one whoop, then more and more filled the air as chairs and furniture were pushed against the walls of what would one day be a creepy-ass sitting room, but for now became a dance floor.

Walt picked up the fiddle, sat on a chair and laid it across his lap instead of tucking it under his chin.

Sadie took up the autoharp and Sarah the dulcimer, which she also held in her lap, long slender hammers in each hand.

"HeyyyyUP!" shouted Tommy, and started picking away like lightning. Sarah and Sadie joined in, and soon boots were stomping and hands were clapping.

But the house really came down when Walt picked up his bow and started sawing his fiddle plumb in half.

"Play it, Walt!" Someone yelled.

"Make that fiddle *talk!*" shouted someone else.

Richard barely saw the bow as it flew across the strings, sending out a reel so fast most of the dancers gave up trying to keep time and just stomped away, big goofy grins on their faces as they yelped and whooped.

"Welt them floorboards!" Walt called. "Shake them trotters!"

Jig followed reel followed Richard didn't know what. He found himself smiling and clapping along, tapping both feet as he sat and drank it all in.

"*Hooray Jack and Hooray John,*" Stub chanted in that mountain singsong that no one from outside ever got quite right.

"*Breakin' up Christmas all night long.*
Way back yonder, long time ago
The old folks danced the do-si-do.
Way down yonder 'longside the creek
I seen Santy Claus warshin' his feet.
Santy Claus come, done and gone,
Breakin' up Christmas right along."

The crowd joined in the second time around, clapping and stomping in unison.

Richard sang too, staring in wonder as his young Pap burned resin and Uncle Tommy's fingers flew over the banjo strings while Granny Earnie beat her dulcimer into submission.

How had he gone his whole life without knowing what his family was capable of?

This might all be a concussion dream, but it was damn fine music for all that.

6

THE SINGING and dancing and playing went on and on as the jugs emptied and the crowd grew more wobbly, until Stub finally laid his banjo aside and started helping usher people back out to their wagons and carts.

"Shew!" Walt said, wiping an arm across his sweaty brow. "That sure was some kind of fun."

"I could listen to you play all night," Sarah said, her own face sweaty and flushed. "Can I help with the cleaning up, Walt? Can I, Mama?"

Sadie and Stub swapped another knowing, resigned glance.

"Well, I reckon we best get this truck loaded back up in the wagon," Stub said. "I'll take Sarah's dulcimer. Richard? Mind to get the fiddle so's we can keep it all together for tomorrow night? Only make sure you don't burn your fingers, it's that red hot from Walt's playin'."

"Don't lose her, now," Walt said, handing the instrument to Richard without looking at him. His eyes were all for Sarah Earnestine. "I'll want her back."

Richard promised to take care, but he doubted Walt or Sarah heard him.

He walked out the door and toward the porch steps, studying the battered, nearly varnish-free fiddle and bow. No Stradivarius, but damn it had sounded great in Walt's hands.

Looking at the fiddle instead of his feet, Richard walked right off the porch a good two feet to the side of the steps.

"Shit!"

He had enough presence of mind to twist his body, holding the fiddle against his chest as he landed flat on his back and his head connected sharply with the frozen ground.

Two lumps in one day, he thought as more red light filled his head. Gotta be some kind of record.

7

"Richard, honey! Wake up!"

Someone was shaking him. Someone heartless and cruel.

He opened his eyes and saw Granny Earnie's wrinkled and tired face framed by the weatherworn porch and white aluminum siding of the house. The steady glow of electric light shone from the windows and open door.

"I'm okay, Granny," Richard said, sitting up and rubbing the new lump on the back of his head. "Just tripped is all."

"Well you give me one booger of a fright," she said, fussing and petting at him as he got carefully to his feet. "Where'd you get that thing? You make it down to town and back after all?"

Richard looked where she was pointing, and saw a battered old fiddle and bow on the frosty earth.

He blinked. Shook his head. Blinked again.

Nope, the fiddle was still there.

Holy sheep shit.

He saw the worry still on Granny's face. Probably made worse by the huge and foolish grin he felt stretching his own.

The watch Stub hadn't yet given to Granny said it was past midnight. Too late to make any phone calls tonight, but he could send an email and leave a voicemail on a certain music store proprietor/bluegrass musician's machine, yesiree he could do that.

"Granny? Would you mind if I invited a few people over tomorrow? I've got a surprise for you and Pap."

8

Matt Blevins had jumped at the suggestion.

"Breakin' up Christmas?" he'd said when Richard finally got him on the phone the next morning. "Geez, I ain't heard that one since I was a kid. My granddad talked about it. Even taught me the tune. But he couldn't remember all the words. You know them?"

Richard promised that he'd sing the words so long as Matt and his band could do the music.

And here they came at two o'clock sharp, after the hospice visit but before the morphine took full hold of Pap.

As they crowded into the sitting room, setting up their gear and going over all that music-y stuff that Richard only half understood, he laid the fiddle on Pap's chest.

"Here you go, Pap," he said as the old man's weak hands came up to cradle the instrument. "You told me to be sure you got her back. Sorry it took me so long."

Light flickered into Pap's eyes. Not much, but some.

Matt had his banjo strapped on and he started picking away. Soon a fiddle and dulcimer joined in.

They were good, but the fire didn't burn near so hot as Richard remembered from last night.

Ah well, beggars can't be choosers.

In the hospital bed, Pap smiled dreamily and pulled the fiddle closer against his bony chest.

"Lord have mercy," Granny said, sticking her head around the doorway. "Is that *Breakin' Up Christmas* y'all are playin'?"

Richard waved her into the room.

"C'mon, Granny," he said, taking her hands and spinning her first left, then right. "Welt them floorboards!"

She laughed and tried to pull her hands away.

But she didn't try too hard.

Richard saw Pap's trembling fingers tapping the fiddle to the beat, and felt his grin get goofier.

"Shake them trotters, Granny!"

"Hooray Jack and Hooray John,
Breakin' up Christmas all night long."

JASON A. ADAMS
Author of Andrew and Shichi-Go-San
ELVES AND
ERGONOMICS

For everyone who appreciates a comfy chair.

1

———————

TINA BRADDOCK COULDN'T WAIT for Christmas Day.

All through the house hung long strings of silver garland and gold tinsel. Every Star Trek ornament Hallmark had ever sold (so far) hung from the living room ceiling, and every card she'd gotten since she was three covered the walls with winter scenes, cartoon characters, and syrupy rhymes.

From the ceiling speakers, Elvis crooned carols. Dolly would follow with her own versions of many of the same songs, before handing the mike to the Mormon Tabernacle Choir. She had over forty hours of her favorite holiday music that played on a loop every year from Black Friday until after the last colorful glass bauble was packed away sometime in January.

Green glass bowls full of tiny air bubbles like frozen foam (the guy at the craft show said they were made from old soda bottles) held her collection of Christmas tree balls. Mostly the plain ones in primary reds, blues, yellows, and greens; but also some mirrored silver and gold, and a few coppery ones she'd found in Santa Claus, Indiana. Those were her favorites, and sat in the bowl next to her desk alongside an antique brass pen holder embossed with snowy Alpine scenery.

Maybe not exactly Christmas, but it fit the mood. And it was the perfect place to keep her working supply of candy canes. The peppermint ones, anyway. The only candy canes worth eating came with red and white stripes and a three-day aftertaste. To hell with all those fancy-schmancy multi-colored neo-canes and their silly fruity flavors.

Sharp peppermint filled the air, competing with pine resin, gingerbread, cocoa, and all the other seasonal stinks of the mouth-watering variety.

The evergreen essence came from the tree in the family room, of course. A beautiful white pine her husband had cut on the far side of Mt. Charleston. It wasn't cone shaped like a traditional tree, but it shouldn't drop needles either, like fur from an exploding cat.

The tree held all of her most special holiday

ornaments. Finds from travels all over the world, and from a dozen different traditions. There were the usual manger-in-a-ball trinkets, found in a Christmas market in Vienna on their honeymoon. Dreidels and tiny silver menorahs from a business trip to Jerusalem several years ago. Bronze strips engraved with Japanese characters she assumed said the equivalent of Merry Christmas, from a tiny church outside Kyoto.

And there were even more business trips planned for the following year. Who knew what all she might find for her next annual Holiday Extravaganza?

Tina's business furniture career had skyrocketed since everyone started working remotely during the darkest days of the COVID plague, and had been growing steadily ever since.

Tina's and her husband's, of course.

Braddock's Home Office Ergonomics had been written up in *Business Weekly, The New York Times,* and *Southern Living*. Not bad for two ex-cube jockeys who'd tired of numb butts and achy backs.

She and her husband Jeff (Crenshaw. She'd kept her own name, thank you very much) had just moved into a classic 1981 split-level at number 43 Carmichael Terrace, on the lower slope of Mt. Charleston, just west of Las Vegas. She didn't care what her friends thought, Tina loved the crazy design of three half-stories stacked on top of each other and overlapping. And a short drive up the road took them to the local version of winter wonderland, and down the way let them enjoy all the city's decorations in their shirt sleeves. Okay, maybe with a light wind-breaker if the night was especially chilly.

For someone who'd grown up in central Illinois, the panic amongst the natives whenever the mercury dropped below forty degrees never failed to amuse.

Jeff loved the house, too. Not so much for its late-twentieth-century aesthetic as for the four-car semi-detached garage. A garage that had absolutely zero room for even *one* car, having been usurped for the esoteric power tools, machine lathes, upholstery gadgets, and other stuff he used to craft the prototype designs for chairs, desks, accessories, and other office furniture they sent out first to reviewers, and then to factories.

Several of the Christmas ornaments most promi-nently displayed had come from Jeff's workshop. When not mucking about with carbon fiber and aircraft aluminum, he enjoyed puttering around with his vintage Shopsmith woodworking gadget, cranking out wooden gewgaws of all sorts, including perfect little miniature versions of their office furniture. Theoretically scale models for client presentations, but the tiny chairs and desks made very nice tree bling with that special in-joke flourish.

Tina loved all of his creations, especially the black walnut icicles he turned on the lathe, and thanked him kindly for each and every one.

But she much preferred the thrill of the hunt. Wandering through dusty old out-of-the-way shops in dusty old out-of-the-way places. Finding the towns where they'd never heard an American accent. Looking for the local version of holiday kitsch.

And acquiring it for her collection.

While Jeff spent his days crafting rolling chairs and convertible sit/stand desks, Tina worked on the website. Marketing plans. Manufacturing arrangements (with factories chosen on the basis of shopping possibilities). Sales meetings with office managers all across the Americas, Great Britain, and the EU.

She never guessed how little that experience would prepare her for her strangest business meeting of all.

2

———————

Two days before Christmas Eve, Tina sat at the sturdy wood-and-steel kitchen table. One of Jeff's designs. He'd started with a raisable workbench from the local DIY emporium, and made his own special modifications and reinforcements until she was pretty sure she could park a Sherman tank on the polished butcher-block top.

Nothing that extreme today, though. Instead, she knelt until her eyes were about four inches from the table's surface, looking across a tableau of 1:10-scale desk chairs, gourmet filing cabinets, and of course, the BHOE-230 Extensible Laptop Station, their latest sit/stand desk design.

Well, *Jeff*'s design. *Her* idea. Mostly.

The prospective client should be here any time, which was perfect. The rich aroma of cinnamon and ginger filled the room, and the oven timer showed five minutes before the gingerbread was due. What's a holiday without fresh gingerbread, she'd like to know? Of course Christmas absolutely required it, but she'd dig in to her own homemade for any holiday. Shucks. World Overweight Gopher Day would do, or any day ending in *y*.

Jeff was down in town prowling through Vegas's surprising number of metal, carbon fiber, and fabric supply houses for anything new, exciting, or on sale. Today was all Tina's show, which she would never admit she preferred. Her hubby was an artist and a genius, but he could put a hyperactive roadrunner to sleep when he started talking shop.

Checking herself in the hall mirror, Tina gave a pat here and a tug there, making sure her festive red pantsuit and green blouse were just so. She'd stopped short of wearing her holly-shaped jewelry, but the silver and gold hoops in her ears still kept her properly decorated.

She'd never heard of the company she was waiting on, *Federated Plaything Delivery Services,* but a quick web search had disabused her of her first reaction. Not a porn trucker, not a pimpmobile fleet.

Not much else to go on, but they were a duly registered freight biz with no dings at the Better Business Bureau, and a legal EIN. She'd offer the rep a piece of gingerbread.

Eh, she'd filled orders for shadier operations. As long as the checks cashed, she let them mind their own beeswax.

Tina adjusted a couple of the tiny chairs, making sure they presented to best effect with the Dolly Dream Desk. The table looked like a setup for the world's lamest role-playing game, but that was all right. She'd loved building and decorating dollhouses her whole life, and who said dolls couldn't earn an honest living out in the workforce?

The dinger on her trusty Kenmore dinged. Tina got her reindeer oven mitts on, opened the door and sucked in a lungful of ginger and molasses goodness, trying not to drool all down her badass-sales-lady pantsuit.

She'd just set the Pyrex pan on a cooling rack when she heard the brass flap of the front door mail slot flapping away.

Her eyebrows came together for a hug as she checked her watch. Ten-thirty in the morning? Saul the Mailman was as punctual as the heartburn from strip-mall Mexican food, and shouldn't be here until one.

Then she perked up. Maybe it was one of the

neighborhood busybodies dropping off Christmas cards!

Rubbing her hands and grinning, Tina walked through to the foyer, reminding herself to get on her own cards for the neighbors, even though they'd have to have generic greetings, since she'd only met a few—

Hm. Nothing on the mat. No envelopes. No packages. Definitely no cards.

A curious critter, maybe?

"Hiya. You must be Miz Braddock. Pleased ta meetcha, ma'am."

Tina squeaked as her heels left the floor.

She spun around, looking for the owner of the voice. The high-pitched voice. Almost as squeaky as the squeak she'd just squeaked.

Nothing. No one. Just the silly elf-on-the-shel...

Huh?

She didn't have any of those nonsensical nannies. She despised the idea that some parents wanted their kids to feel like they were prisoners under the watchful eyes of creepy little guards.

The four-inch-tall elf on the shelf stood up then, and offered its wee hand.

"Sassafras O'Poole," he...it...said. "Field purchasing agent first class, FPDS Mojave District. Nice suit, by the way. Red's *every*one's color."

"Uh...um..." Tina gawped at the figure standing on her foyer knickknack shelf, right between last year's card from the Nelsons (Rockwell Santa scene) and the one from her grandparents (2004, photo of Poppa and Mamaw in matching reindeer sweaters, storebought grins, and Santa hats).

Red bellbottoms hung down over little black, elastic-sided Chelsea boots. Above, the elf...she supposed it *must* be an elf, what else would it be... wore a matching red pocket polo with broad lapels and a teensy pocket protector full of even teensier pens. No white fur trimming, but she saw *FPDS* stitched on the pocket in swirls of incredibly fine gold and silver thread. Pointy ears, pointy nose, even a pointy chin. All below lips as red as his shirt, which complimented rather than clashed with the bright blue ducktail hair and sideburns.

"Don't tell me I got the wrong addy," the elf, Sassafras, said, dropping his (no bumps on the chest, so *his* seemed safe) hand. "I was a delivery donkey for three hunnert and forty years before I took the office job. I know a 43 Carmichael Terrace when I see it."

Tina shook her head couple of times. First to clear it, then again when the elf's question finally registered.

"No. Not at all, Mr...ah...Mr? O'Poole. I mean, yes, this is 43."

"Yeah, I thought so. But call me Sassy. So whatcha got to show me, Miz B?"

Really, the only sensible thing to do in this completely *un*-sensible situation was what she did best.

"Oh, yes. Of course. Please, call me Tina. You're interested in viewing BHOE's *Madison* collection. A rather nice improvement over last year's *Charleston* line. I have some samples ready, if you'll follow me."

"With those stems?" A squeaky laugh. "Lady, you'd leave me in the dust."

Sassy hopped off the shelf, and was suddenly perched on Tina's shoulder, hanging on to a gold hoop earring like a commuter on the bus and giving off the faint lemony aroma of Brylcream.

Tina returned to the kitchen, ridden by Sassy the Elf and a nagging suspicion some illegal pharmaceutical or other had been slipped into her morning oatmeal. She gestured toward the miniature tableau on the table.

"As you can see, Mr.—Sassy, I mean—Braddock's Home Office Ergonomics has everything you might need to—"

"Hey, now," Sassy said, jumping from her shoulder to the table. "I gotta try me a piece of *this* baby!"

He skittered (that was the only word for it, his

tiny legs were a blur) to a miniature chair nearly as tall as he was and with a sigh like a teakettle winding up, settled into a reclining, mesh-backed and tush-cushioned luxury that would have been at home on any starship's bridge.

"This...now *this* is what I'm talkin' about!" he said, rubbing the baby-soft beige acrylic fabric on the armrests. "A field buyer's bum could fall in love with this beauty."

In spite of the general weirdness of the situation, Tina couldn't help the pleased smile that eased her facial muscles.

"Mr...Sassy, you have excellent taste. That is the BHOE-9500, the finest desk chair on the market for those who will be sitting for long periods. May I?"

She leaned forward and used a fingernail to press one of the many levers under the seat, which promptly switched the chair from static to reclinable.

"Oh yeah...nice," Sassy said, rocking and closing his eyes. "Really nice, you know what I'm saying?"

Opening one of the kitchen table's drawers, Tina pulled out a sheaf of full-color brochures, spec sheets, and price lists.

"And that's only one of the sixteen adjustments you can make on this particular model," she said, before lining up the other chairs in order of complexity (and cost). "All of our seating is built to precise standards. All guaranteed for ten years of normal use."

She spread the materials out, opening the brochures so Sassy wouldn't have to try and wrangle paper twice as long as he was. She supposed he'd have to walk the words.

"Oh my," she said, popping her forehead with one hand as Sassy took what appeared to be a set of Sassy-sized reading glasses from his pocket. "Where are my manners?"

While her potential client perused the documentation, Tina plucked a stainless-steel spatula from a repurposed Bavarian stein covered with winter scenes and used it to cut the fresh gingerbread into two-inch squares. She set one of the middle squares on a plate for herself, but offered the coveted corner piece to Sassy.

The corner piece which was waist-high to the elf-sized elf.

"Oh, dear," she said. "I wasn't thinking. I'll cut it into smaller pieces for you."

"Keep your knickers untwisted," Sassy said with a grin. "Ain't nothin' gonna keep yours truly from snarfin' down good gingerbread."

With that, he began tearing into the still-steaming slice, his tiny arms as blurry as his legs had been, stuffing each handful into his mouth.

In less than thirty seconds, all eight cubic inches of brown bliss had disappeared.

Sassy gave an almost human-volume belch.

"Beg pardon," he said, licking his fingers and not looking the least bit embarrassed. "Tina, if the rest of your stuff is as good as that gingerbread and my new chair, I think we can do some business."

Hallucination or not, Tina felt a flush of pride. She did make a mean gingerbread, if she did say so herself. And that "my new chair" bit made her think she might have made a sale today.

"So how many of these other chairs ya got?" he said, hopping back into the 9500 and waving a hand at the line of lower-end models. "This one here is already spoken for."

"How many?" Tina realized this particular client might present a challenge. "Well, I'm afraid what you see is all we have of these particular sizes. These are only demonstration models. We never planned on customers as...I mean, most of our clients are around my size."

Sassy grinned up at her, still fondling the armrests.

"I'm just yankin' your chain, sister. I know you wasn't thinkin' of guys like me when you set up shop."

He pointed out three of the brochures.

"You gimme the specs and blueprints—*exact* blueprints and specs, mind, materials included—for the 9200 and 9000 models, scaled to match the showroom pieces. Me and my folks will take care of manufacturin'. And you guys get paid full price for each unit we produce. Direct transfer to your account, so no worries about convertin' bullion to cash. Deal?"

"You have manufacturing facilities for furniture?" Then she gulped a little gulp.

Bullion?

Now Sassy's grin turned into a laugh that tinkled like sleighbells. It was the oddest laugh she'd ever heard, but after all, he *was* an elf.

"Oh, we got us some great fabricators," he said, getting back to his feet. "The best. And all union, all the time. You want, I can arrange for you and your hubs to visit the shop. Might want to pick up somethin' warmer than the pants, though."

Sassy put his hands on top of the 9500's (multi-adjustable) headrest and pressed down, compressing the extremely strong and durable chair until he could put it in his pocket. There had *definitely* been something in that oatmeal this morning.

"I'll have to get Jeff to make copies of his design sheets," she said, wondering if it was too early in the day to add a splash of rum to her post-meeting eggnog. "He's the artisanal side of things. I'll...um, do you have a fax or email or mailing address?"

"Just leave the stuff under your Christmas tree," Sassy said, bounding off the table onto the floor and blur-walking his way toward the front door and its mail slot. "We'll send someone around to pick it up tomorrow. Merry ho-ho and all that jazz!"

With one last flap, Sassy the Elf was gone, along with her only demo model of the BHOE-9500 Executive Special.

Tina stared at the still-wobbling brass flap, her eyebrows hugging again as she tried to decide what, if anything, had actually happened.

But the 9500 was gone.

So was one of her beloved gingerbread corners.

She'd just added that splash of rum to a tall glass of homemade eggnog when her cell phone beeped its new-text beep. Jeff letting her know he was home-ward bound.

Tina hit speed dial and waited for her genius artist to answer.

"Hey, honey," she said, a goofy grin spoiling her badass-businesswoman mystique. "I hope you're ready for a really interesting Christmas surprise."

JASON A. ADAMS

Author of Andrew and Shichi-Go-San

A True Family Holiday

For the misfits who find a place to fit in.

1

CARRIE GAVE sigh of relief when she saw the steel screens rattling down over the store's mall-side entrance.

Five days until Christmas, and the Northlake Mall Sears had been the scene of screaming toddlers, fighting couples, desperate husbands, harried wives. Men with wedding rings staring at her tits and making vile suggestions, and a work policy that said she had to be cheerful and polite no matter what.

The people clashed with maniacally cheerful lights and decorations, animatronic elves, three (count 'em!) Santas competing over who could sneak the most booze in between terrified children peeing on their waterproof Santa pants.

A last quick till count, and she could escape this horrid place and get back to her quiet and people-free apartment. She loved living in Atlanta, had since she first moved here six months ago, but she still wasn't used to how many people filled the city. A far cry from Mountain City, Tennessee.

And she was four hours from her family, which worked out nicely.

Carrie finished off her tepid, bitter Starbucks, grateful she'd opted for plain old coffee instead of one of the holiday sugar bombs. She didn't think she could have tolerated room temperature Candy Cane Snowball Reindeer Delight, or whatever the silly drink *du jour* was.

The store went blessedly quiet, or at least quiet*er*, when the Muzak system stopped pounding out oppressively cheerful Christmas carols. Carrie had hated those songs since she was a kid, and wondered why, in a place as culturally diverse as Atlanta, no one thought to sprinkle in a Chanukah tune or two.

Although listening to the Dreidel song over and over again might not be any better.

Carrie's feet, legs, and back ached, and she could smell herself when she pulled the cash drawer from the overworked register. The desk job hadn't prepared her for this.

A graphic designer by trade, she'd decided to pick up some extra cash—and a good excuse—

working retail for the holidays. Double- and triple-time Sears wages didn't match what she made with a computer, but every little bit helped.

One particularly horrible couple were ushered toward the door by Lenny. Like herself, he was a seasonal employee. But he'd been hired for his mass. Lenny was a minor league (or whatever) pro wrestler who worked security in between pratfalls. Carrie like to tease him about the "reality" of pro wrestling, but he was a genuinely nice guy for all his Evil Wrestler stage act.

Still, no one stayed rowdy or refused to leave when six-and-a-half-feet of nearly silent mohawked African-American fury got down in their face and quietly asked them to comply with instructions.

He'd once picked her up over his head like she weighed nothing, and given her a helicopter twirl. She'd been scared, delighted, laughing like a crazy woman...and more than a little excited. She wished she wasn't so shy. Lenny didn't wear any rings, and never talked about a significant other.

And my goodness, how he did fill out a tight black t-shirt.

"An ass like that oughtta be illegal, if it's not open to the public."

Carrie jumped, blushing as she turned to see Edward standing beside her, staring thoughtfully as

Lenny continued dragging shoppers to the parking lot exit out by Women's. He was close to her own height, maybe a shade closer to six feet than she was. An impeccable dresser, today he wore a pin-striped shirt with thin, polished leather suspenders. The suspenders held up a pair of zoot suit-style pants, tight-waisted and flaring out like balloons before gripping his ankles like a vise.

"Hey, Edward. You already close out Cosmetics?" She finished counting her drawer. The cash went into a bank bag with the count sheet, and she carried it toward the manager's office.

"Yeah, like half an hour ago," Edward said walking with her. "The rabble stayed away after seven-thirty or so. The sample spritzers got a little *too* dedicated this evening. It got so bad I had to toss my contact lenses. I wouldn't strike a match anywhere near the perfume counter if I was you. You've got it lucky up here in teeny-bopper clothing."

She laid the bank bag on a growing pile in the boss's office, and walked with Edward through the back to the employee's door. All she wanted was some greasy fast food, a nice cup of chamomile tea with a bourbon bracer, and bad movies in bed.

2

———

SHE DID *NOT* WANT a flat tire.

Edward rubbed her shoulders as she looked down at the sadly deflated rubber on her Outback's rear wheel. All the way down. It looked like a napping bloodhound's jowls.

Carrie opened the trunk and checked the empty well. Nope, the spare that had been missing when she bought the old clunker was still gone. So much for Christmas magic.

"Let me give you a ride, sugar," Edward said, as Carrie's throat tightened up. This was one thing too much at the end of an endless shift.

"That's okay," she said, sniffing. "I'll just call a t-t-t-tow..."

And that was it. The next moment she had her

209

head buried in her friend's shoulder while he held and rocked her sobbing body.

"Hey...hey, now... It's not that bad, sweetie. I can take you home. We'll get the Sears-O-Matic people in Auto Service to fix you up tomorrow. Be good as new."

"But I'm not working tomorrow," Carrie said, pulling out of Edward's arms and swiping furiously at her eyes. "I've got to finish a poster and flyers for Spencer's Travel. It's going to take me all day!"

"Work? On the Saturday before Christmas? Tsk, tsk, tsk. That won't do at all, my little sugarplum."

Edward stood, arms crossed, tapping his chin with one finger while he looked toward the sky. Carrie knew that look. He was plotting and scheming again.

"Oh no you don't," she said, pinching his shoulder. "It's late and I'm tired. No bars, no dance clubs!"

"Perish the thought! I think you deserve a night off. But, since I'll be running you back and forth tomorrow, at least until we get your tire fixed, I think you should accept my most generous offer of dinner, drinks, and the sofa bed."

Carrie started to say no, that she really needed to start on that poster early, but Edward had already taken her hand and was steering her toward an over-sized Ford pickup truck. Not the sort of vehicle anyone would expect a guy like Edward to drive, but he called it his only holdover from a childhood in Outer Redneckia.

"Thanks, Edward," she said, taking a tissue from her bag and honking loudly. "I can't tell you how much I appreciate this. Burger King good for you? My treat."

"Absolutely. I love me some Whopper with my vodka."

Carrie laughed, surprising herself. This was why she loved Edward. He could make her smile no matter what else was going on. And he never tried to hit on her.

They swung through a handy drive-through and bought a ridiculous amount of food. Burgers, fries, onion rings, one of each dessert. A quick stop at the package store for two bottles of Grey Goose, and they wound their way through the Atlanta traffic back to Edward's townhouse.

Carrie hauled the bags while Edward opened the door and killed the burglar alarm. She looked around, curious to see how her friend lived. They'd met three weeks ago at store orientation, and hit it off immediately. Kindred spirits, as he said.

The townhouse was another surprise. Spotlessly clean, decorated with Marvel and DC toys, movie posters from a million drive-in creature features, heavily decorated brass vases and hookahs like something out of Arabian Nights...

And not a single holiday decoration. No tree, no tinsel, no lights.

She was about to ask him about that, when her phone buzzed in her pocket. She took it out and saw "MOM" flashing on the screen. Great. Just exactly what she needed to top the day off.

"Hi, Mom," she said, preemptively rubbing her forehead. "What's up?"

"Oh, hello dear! I'm just checking on my little chicken. Have you changed your mind about coming home for Christmas? You know everyone wants to see you."

"Mom, I told you. I have to work through the holidays. Plus, I just got a big contract to do advertising materials for—"

"That's nice, Car-Car. Oh, did I tell you about your brother's promotion? He's going to be foreman at the furniture plant! Isn't that exciting? And your nephews are just *loving* hockey. They're so talented and smart and—"

Carrie tuned the rest out until Edward came back from the kitchen with burgers on plates, fries and rings in bowls, plus a bottle and two shot glasses.

"Gotta run. A friend and I are at dinner and the food just showed up."

"Hi, Mom!" Edward called, dropping Carrie a wink. "Let me have Carrie back, and I promise to return her in good condition."

"Oh, is that a *boy* I hear? I'm so glad, Car-Car. You really need to get—"

"Bye, Mom. I'll call you tomorrow or next day." Carrie disconnected, and flopped back on the couch.

"Please tell me one of those glasses is mine."

"Absolutely, sweetie. Want me to go fetch a tumbler instead?"

"No, I'll be okay. It's just that... I don't know. I love my mom and the family, I guess, but she's never interested in *me*. It's always my brother this and her grandchildren that and did you hear about your cousin Sonnie and. And. And."

"So you're not going home for the holidays, I take it?"

"Are you kidding?" Carrie grabbed a handful of fries and the shotglass Edward had so kindly filled. "My people can be decent enough one-on-one. Some of them, anyway. But get the Holbrook clan together in a large group and things go bad. Dad and my uncles get toasted and start fighting. All the women talk about is how terrible their lives are. Mom...well, you heard. Preacher Price will come by to bless everyone and bless everyone out. Real fire and brimstone and God loves you but you're gonna burn type. I hate all the holidays, but Christmas is the worst."

"I get you, sugar," Edward said, sitting beside Carrie and putting an arm around her. "You should meet my clan. Or maybe it's Klan with a K. My mom and pop love me too, but they never stop worrying about my eternal soul, no matter how many times I tell them I'm not going to a re-education gulag."

3

It was the best evening Carrie'd had in a long time. She and Edward talked the sun up, getting steadily more sloshed and honest as the night went on. They ate bad food, drank, and skipped the bad movies in favor of discussing their reasons for staying away from any sort of family gathering.

Finally, Carrie fell asleep.

Or passed out.

Whatever.

She clawed her way back to consciousness some time later, and immediately regretted it. Cruel light streamed through a crack in the drapes, shoving right through her lids, skewering her eyeballs and brain. Her tongue felt coated in coarse fur. From roadkill, judging by the taste. Someone kept beating on her head with a mallet.

"Up and at 'em, sunshine!" Oh god.

She peeled one eye open. A blurry Edward stood in front of her, a steaming plate of scrambled eggs and toast in one hand, a glass full of red froth in the other.

"Go 'way," she mumbled, burrowing deeper into the couch cushions. She'd somehow acquired a quilt, which she pulled up over her aching head.

"Sorry, girl. Time's a-wastin', and you need some of Edward Campbell's Magic Hangover Cure."

She heard him set the plate and glass on the coffee table, then the blanket was whipped away.

Edward finally badgered her into sitting up and drinking the crimson liquid. A Bloody Mary, but with a bitter undertone.

"Yuck! What's in this? Rat poison?"

"Nope, but I did crush up a couple of tablets of somethin'-somethin'. I have a pharmacist friend who slips me the occasional goodie. Don't worry," he said, holding up a hand. "It's nothing that bad. Perfectly legal when prescribed by a doctor."

And the clamp around her temples *was* easing a bit. She decided to brave the eggs, and realized she was starving. Five minutes later, the glass and the plate were empty.

"Thanks Edward," she said, glancing at her

watch. "I appreci—oh, shit! Noon? I've got to go! I have to work—"

"Tut, tut. Don't you worry, my little chickadee. Doctor Eduardo snooped in your purse and found the travel agent's card. You have been reported as too ill to function, and the deadline has been pushed back a couple of days."

Carrie wished she could manage a grin that smug.

"Okay, thanks I guess. Did you call a tow truck, too?"

"All in good time. Today is a day for celebrating. I'm taking you someplace special, sweetie." The smug kept getting thicker.

"Where?" she asked, growing more suspicious.

"A nice family gathering to celebrate the holidays."

"No. *Hell* no! We talked about all that last night, or at least I think we did. I don't want my family anywhere nearby right now!"

Edward pulled her to her feet. "Not your birth family, sugar. Just wait. You'll understand. But first, girl needs some quality time with a bar of soap. Shew!"

Curious in spite of her misgivings, Carrie took Edward up on the shower, and stepped out feeling more like a living creature. Whatever had been in that drink had kicked the hangover to the curb, thank goodness. She got dressed, combed her fingers through her damp hair, and went back out to the living room.

"There she is! That's the Carrie we all know and love."

"Stow it, clown. So what's this mystery gathering all about?"

"You'll see," he said, dropping another wink. "Get your bag and let's go."

4

EDWARD DROVE THROUGH DECATUR, and then into Druid Hills. Past houses coated with decorations: Christmas, Chanukah, Kwanzaa, and some she didn't recognize. They finally stopped in front of a large Craftsman, completely undecorated except for a green bulb in the porch light.

"Here we are," he said, killing the truck's engine. "Mind your step getting down, and follow me."

He led her up to the heavy walnut door. Carrie heard music and voices from inside, but it all sounded cheerful. No one was yelling, nothing was breaking.

Edward knocked, then rang the bell. Nothing happened.

"Can't hear us," he said. "No worries." He turned

the knob, pushed the door open, and led Carrie into holiday chaos.

"Welcome to your new family home!" he yelled over all the noise.

Carrie stopped in the doorway, goggling. The house was filled with people of all colors, dressed in a dizzying array of clothing. Pale goths covered with Wiccan jewelry, sandy-skinned people in djellabas, some in t-shirts and jeans. Towering over the others, Lenny walked toward Carrie and Edward, wearing a multi-colored dashiki.

"Hey, little girl," Lenny said, wrapping his giant arms around Carrie and swinging her around. "You come to join the family?"

"Family?" she gasped, a little breathless. From the hug.

"Welcome home, honey!" said a woman with flaming red hair, green eyes. She was wearing lederhosen. "I'm Kristen. Kris to my family, and that means you. You must be Carrie. Edward's told us *so* much about you!"

"My girl's the next big advertising honcho!" Lenny said, still keeping Carrie's feet off the ground. "Eddie tells me you scored a big graphics deal with that travel agent over in Buckhead!"

"Put me down, you big goof!" she said, laughing

and slapping Lenny's arms. "Someone needs to tell me what's going on!"

"Look around and see, sweetie," Edward said. He took her by the hand again and led her through rooms full of happy people. Full of decorations. Santa statues, Star Trek Hallmark ornaments, Menorahs, Kwanzaa cards... Even a plain aluminum Festivus pole in one corner. A kid wearing a yarmulke stood chatting and drinking with an older man in a cassock. Pentacles, crucifixes, dreidels, even a three-foot-tall Krampus doll. The place looked like the Amazon Holiday page had drunk a bottle of ipecac.

"You're in Atlanta, honey," Edward said. Lenny and the redhead nodded. "This is the Island of Misfit Boys. And Girls."

"We all got our reasons for not going home," Lenny said, filling a cup with eggnog from a huge crystal punch bowl and handing it to Carrie. She knocked it back in one.

"You can tell us your story or not," Kris said, stroking Carrie's cheek. "Just know that one of the benefits of turning eighteen is you aren't stuck with your biological relatives any more."

"That's right," Edward said. "Everyone here decided at one time or another to upgrade the family situation."

Lenny set Carrie down, and took one of her shaking hands in his giant mitt.

"Home's where you decide it is," Lenny said, stroking the back of her hand with his thumb. "And the best family is the one you choose for yourself."

"We all get together the last Saturday before Christmas for a big, *happy* family get-together," Edward said, taking Carrie's other hand. "We all bring whatever holiday with us, but we celebrate all of them. Or none of them. We celebrate each other, mostly. We call it *Verum Familia*, True Family."

"That's right," said Kris. "Everyone here is special. Everyone here thinks *you're* special, Carrie. We all love you just the way you are. Will you stay and be part of my family?"

"And mine," Edward said.

"And mine?" Lenny said, voice much too soft for the huge body it came from. "Please say yes, sugarbear."

Carrie looked from one face to another.

Friends she knew, friends she'd just met, and friends she hadn't been introduced to yet.

No, not friends. Family.

A family that knew she had a big client.

A family looking at *her*.

That cared how *she* was.

Something pricked the corners of her eyes, and

she noticed she was grinning like an idiot. She hugged first Edward, then Kris. Then she tried to squeeze the life out of Lenny.

She finally let the wrestler go and wiped her cheeks, still smiling.

"Got any more of that eggnog?"

JASON A. ADAMS
Ginger Magic

To all those who bake their way into our hearts.

Home is where you hang your head.

That wasn't really fair, but Ellen Daughtry felt anything but fair as she carried a far-too-empty suit-case in one hand and Pebbles's leash in the other.

Pebbles, her brindled mini-tank of a pibble, walked slowly at Ellen's right ankle, nose and tail nearly dragging the cracked cement of her grandparents' front walk. She was a dog who did *not* like new and exciting things, thank you very much. Ellen hated that she'd had to uproot the poor thing from what she knew and drag her to this strange place.

Pebbles had only been with Ellen for a few months, and this was the first time they'd be sleeping somewhere besides the comfortable memory-foam mattress in the tidy little Atlanta apartment.

Ellen was coming home to Green Cove, a tiny

town snuggled in amongst the Appalachian ridges of Virginia, but poor Pebbles was not. Pebbles was a city girl, much like Ellen had tried to become.

The ancestral Daughtry manse waited at the end of the walk; a century-old double-decker Craftsman with about a mile of twinkling lights wrapped around the stocky, tapering porch columns. A couple of plastic Frostys flanked the porch steps, and would be casting their inner LED glow across the still-green fescue once the sun went down and the power bill went up. In the yard, a troop of Santas wearing costumes from at least four different countries faced her with their creepy frozen smiles.

Always reminded her a little of that damn clown doll from *Poltergeist.*

But Pop loved his decorating. Now that seventy was in his rearview, he'd scaled down. A little. No sleigh and reindeer on the roof, no maniacal elves up in the naked branches of the titanic red oak that, when dressed in its spring and summer leaves, shaded the entire front lawn.

But what he could still attack had suffered the brunt of his holiday glee.

And with two weeks to go before Christmas Day, he still had plenty of festooning time. Which would keep him out of Grammy's hair as she processed a plantation's worth of sugar into holiday cookies, pies, cakes, and all the other stuff that kept dentists and endocrinologists in business.

Probably all ginger-based, this time of the season.

Grammy always pulled out all the stops for the town's Gingers and Breads festival, an annual gorge-fest of All Things Ginger, including the chefs. Tomorrow was the big day, and Grammy would bake until the roosters crowed, if Ellen knew her at all.

To enter the contest, the baker had to be a bona fide redhead. Plenty of those to be found among the local descendants of Scots-Irish immigrants, but town rumor held that anyone thought to have a store-bought carrot top would be pulled into the sheriff's office to prove the carpet matched the drapes.

With her own locks the color of well-aged walnut, Ellen had never been able to compete, although she'd always loved helping Grammy bake up her own entries.

In spite of Ellen's gloom, the aromas of woodsmoke drifting down from the tall age-darkened river-rock chimney mixed with the mouthwatering scent of molasses and spices from a kitchen window open to combat the heat of oven and stove to tug at her inner greedy little kid.

And at her memories of simpler times, back before...

Well, *before.*

She and Pebbles barely got a foot on the first step before the screen door *spronked* open and Pop, Ellen's granddad, appeared, a pair of antlers jutting up above his unkempt gray mop. And above a *truly* hideous red and green sweater that showed a bleary-eyed red-nosed reindeer blowing into a breathalyzer.

"Hey, Punkin! I thought that might be your Tokyoter pullin' up. Get yourself on in here, girl!"

Fred Daughtry might be getting up in years, but he'd lost none of the zest for life that Ellen used to have herself. He positively bounded across the Astro-turfed porch boards, yanked the battered black Samsonite from her hand, and bent down to pat Pebbles.

For her part, Pebbles allowed the touch, but whined and hunched up. Not her fault. She wasn't good with people.

Another failure. Ellen hadn't done a good enough job socializing Pebbles. Too busy trying to get ahead at Duke & Wilson, the law firm she'd joined right after passing the Georgia Bar exam.

The law firm that had cut her loose, along with most of the other underlings. *After* she'd bought a brand-new Camry, and *after* she'd laid down first, last, and security on a two-bedroom in a brand-new building a block away from Decatur's courthouse square.

It had taken Ellen exactly one month to realize she wouldn't be able to keep both apartment and car once her first few job leads didn't pan out.

And so here she was, running back home with no job, no money, and no prospects. Just a new car, the jeans and UVA sweatshirt she wore plus a few changes of clothes, and a four-legged child to feed.

She wondered if Jack Buchanan still needed help from time to time. He'd been the one who helped get her a free-ride scholarship to UVA Law, and who'd given her her first internship before she moved down to Atlanta to—hah!—make her fortune.

Pop and Grammy had jumped at the chance to take care of her while she hunted for work, of course. But dammit, they shouldn't have to!

"Hey, Pop," she said, and leaned down to scratch her dog's block of a head. "It's okay, Pebbles girl. Pop's one of the good ones."

"You don't have to tell the poor thing lies, Ellie."

Pop laughed as Grammy came through the door, wiping flour all over a stained kitchen towel. She wore her usual baby-blue knit slacks, along with a faded shirt decorated with Pink Floyd's prism on the front. Her long gray hair only had a streak or two of copper left, but pale skin and a liberal coating of freckles kept her qualifications for the Gingers and Breads bakeoff from ever being questioned.

"You bring me some sugar, Sugar?" Pop said. He wrapped his free arm around Grammy's plump waist and smacked her a wet one on the cheek. She swatted him with her towel, sending up a white cloud of flour as she giggled like a tween.

"You stop all that foolishness, Fred Daughtry! You'll put the blush on me, and whatever will Ellie's girl think of me then?"

Ellie's girl was currently pressed against her mama's legs, trembling and staring up at these two demented strangers with wide eyes.

Grammy pushed Pop away, then bent down with her hands on her knees.

"Little girl's just nervous about the new, is all," she said, then fished in the pocket of her slacks and pulled out a dark brown disk as thick as Ellen's little finger. Grammy held it out at full arm's length toward Pebbles, who sniffed cautiously toward her hand.

"C'mon now, little girlie," Grammy crooned. "It's okay. Just a sample from some gingersnaps that spent a tad too much time in the oven."

Pebbles inched forward one slow paw at a time, and carefully plucked the cookie from Grammy's fingers. Loud crunching and lip-smacking ensued, and Ellen was surprised and pleased to see Pebbles sniff Grammy's fingers, tail still low but wagging now.

"There now," Grammy said as she straightened. "I can tell you and me are going to be good friends, ain't we girl?"

Ellen winced as Pebbles wagged her whiptail harder, welting the back of her knee with each swipe.

A low roar rose down the street, slowly getting louder as it came closer. Ellen saw an oversized and battered white pickup truck approaching, a holly wreath wired to the grille and the bed piled up past the cab's roof with split firewood.

"Oh, hey," Pop said. "Perfect timing. Let me get your bag inside, Ellie, then you can help me and Deke unload the wood."

Grammy held the door for Pop, Ellen, and Pebbles, then took the leash.

"Fred can't split like he used to could," Grammy said. "Deke Gantry keeps the woodstove fed these days, plus takes care of all the other chores your Pop likes to ignore."

"Pshaw," Pop said, taking off his reindeer antlers and picking up a pair of leather work gloves from the landing table beside the door. "I just like to help the local entrepreneurs when I can, Dory." He gave Ellen a wink, and Grammy a tweak on the tush, earning himself another giggle and swat. "C'mon,

Ellie. Let's show that young man where to park his load."

Pebbles had been siren-songed by another ginger-snap, so Ellen sighed and followed Pop back outside, where he opened the side gate and waved toward the truck. She felt like Pebbles, not interested in meeting anyone new.

The overloaded truck turned in and drove around behind the house and the engine died. The door opened, and Ellen missed her next couple of breaths.

The driver of the truck—Deke Gantry, she supposed—hopped down and stretched, leaning back with his arms in a wide vee over his head.

Fine arms, too. Ellen could see where his green plaid flannel stretched over his shoulders and biceps. While the man wasn't as musclebound as a pro body-builder, he had all the hard lines of someone who, well, split and hauled firewood for a living.

It was when he dropped his arms and looked at her with eyes as blue as glacier ice that she forgot how to breathe altogether.

Those eyes went just right with shoulder-length curls as red as sin and just as wild. A bushy moun-tain-man beard covered the lower part of his face, but not enough to hide full lips that curled into a smile when Pop walked over to shake his hand.

That smile could get a girl in trouble. Probably.

"Heya, Deke! Glad you're here. Ol' Bessie's been gobblin' the wood this year. I think she's sprung a leak or three around the window gasket. Oh, by the way. This here's Ellie. Ellen, I mean." He leaned toward the big man and said in a ridiculously loud stage whisper, "She's all growed up, you know."

Heat climbed Ellen's cheeks, even as she couldn't help but laugh. Pop would never get too old to be a little kid.

Deke laughed, too. A nice laugh. Not loud, not reserved, but just right. The laugh of a man who knew how.

He retrieved his hand from Pop and held it out her way.

"Deacon Gantry," he said. "Deke. Mighty pleased to meet you, Miss Daughtry. Or is it Mrs. something else?"

His voice, smooth and smoky as good scotch, lit up her goosebumps and did interesting things inside her belly.

"Not Mrs. anything," she said, "Just Ellen is fine." She took his hand. And nearly snatched her own back at the jolt she felt in his gentle handshake.

She wasn't a bit displeased at the way his own eyes went wide, either.

Ellen wasn't sure how long a handshake between

strangers was supposed to last, but Pop's cough brought her back down somewhere close to earth.

"Say, I'd best go check up on Dory, see if she needs any help in the kitchen. Whyn't you two young'uns get all that wood unloaded and stacked up against the house?" He pointed to where the remnants of the last wood delivery lay against the wall beside the kitchen door, then all but skipped back inside.

Ellen watched him go, realized she still had hold of Deke's hand, and looked back at him just in time for both of them to bust out laughing.

2

———

DEKE HAD NEVER ENJOYED STACKING wood so much.

Ellen Daughtry was something else. She had to look up to see his eyes, but not too far. Neither slim nor stout, she had a curvy and fit figure that filled out a pair of faded jeans in all the right places. Hard to tell what her baggy college sweatshirt might be hiding, but a little mystery was fine by him.

Sharp as a new tack, too. And with a wicked sense of humor that kept catching him off guard. He dropped more than one armload when she snuck up with a comment that shook the laugh right out of him.

"Have we met before?" she asked as they dropped their last loads onto the neatly stacked cord row and pulled a blue nylon tarp over to keep the damp and snow off. "I thought I knew just about everyone my age in this town."

"I don't believe so." Deke stretched his arms forward, up, and back, easing out the kinks. "I grew up over in Mason County, and went to school in Haytersville. I didn't move here to Green Cove until last April. I feel like I've met *you*, though. I recognize you from all those pictures lining Mr. and Mrs. D's hallway. You sure were a cute kid."

Ellen rolled her eyes as more color rose to join the work-apples in her cheeks, but she looked pleased all the same.

And had she been checking him out while he stretched? Nah.

"Come on inside," she said. "Grammy always keeps a pitcher of the world's best iced tea in the fridge, and December or not, I've worked up a sweat and a thirst."

Deke didn't need much persuading. He'd had the pleasure of Mrs. D's tea many a time, and with any luck they could sneak a nibble of whatever was smelling the place up so nice. Some of her damned fine gingersnaps, if his nose told the truth.

With a swipe of his steel-toes across the mud brush and a wipe of his hands on his pocket rag, Deke felt decent enough to hold the door for Ellen, who batted her long, dark lashes at him like a black-and-white movie vixen.

"Why, *thank* you, kind sir."

He laughed and followed her into a kitchen overflowing with candy canes, holly, red ribbon, and luscious goodies.

"My very great honor and pleasure, madame."

Inside, Mrs. D puttered and fussed her way between pantry, stove, table, and oven. There was indeed a pan of still-steaming ginger cookies reeking of molasses and cranking up Deke's drool factory. Also a square glass dish holding gingerbread dark with blackstrap and dusted with just the right amount of powdered sugar.

Deke put his hands in his pockets like his dad had taught him to do whenever temptation reared its ugly head. The old bastard hadn't been worth much, but that lesson was still a good one.

"How many things you entering in the G&B this year, Mrs. D?"

"Just the snaps and the gingerbread this year," she said, grinding black pepper into a mixing bowl. "And you'd best not be making notes, young man. My gingerbread recipe ain't for nobody but Ellie, and that's only after I'm in a box. Fred! You touch one more gingersnap and I'll wale the skin right off your bones!"

Mr. D dropped the cookie he'd been holding and snatched his hands behind his back, grinning sheepishly and looking like the world's oldest five-year-old.

"Just checkin' the bake, Dory. Wanna make sure it's up to snuff."

Mrs. D popped him in the butt with her kitchen rag. "I'll snuff *you*, you old fool. But you can have *one* snap, if you take another one in yonder to Miss Pebbles."

Through the door between kitchen and sitting room, Deke saw a tan and brown tiger-striped pit bull laying on her side on the hearth mat in front of Ol' Bessie, a pitch-black hunk of cast iron probably as old as the house. The dog's eyes were closed and she had a suspicious bulge in the midsection, but her long, skinny tail thumped the mat a couple of times at the sound of her name.

"Um," Ellen said, pouring tea from a knobbly green pitcher into two equally knobbly green tumblers. "Exactly how many gingersnaps has she gotten? Will she need to go on a diet?"

Mrs. D's dimples came out to play as she smiled.

"Oh, only but a few. She's too skinny, you know."

Ellen's eyes, nearly as dark as Mrs. D's gingerbread, rolled again.

"Grammy, I swear. You never spoiled *me* nearly so much."

Mrs. D glanced Deke's way and gave a wink that let him know Ellen might be fibbing just a little. Then she took a shiny and well-seasoned cast iron skillet down from a nail on the wall.

"You two done worked off your breakfast, I'm sure," she said, setting the pan on a free stove eye before taking ham, eggs, milk, and a couple of boxes from the icebox. "Why don't you all go sit with Miss Pebbles and let me fix you up a little something to eat? Go on, now. Shoo yourselves out from under my feet."

Chased by a flapping rag, Deke and Ellen escaped to the sofa and flopped down, laughing some more.

God, he could bury himself inside her laugh and die happy.

His own laugh cut off when Pebbles opened her eyes enough to see him.

The pit bull sprang to her feet with a petite poot that didn't go well with her cringing whine as her tail drooped and she backed away, nearly singeing her butt on the rocket-hot stove.

"Pebbles! Settle down, girlie." Ellen leaned forward and snapped her fingers lightly, patiently coaxing the terrified pooch until she crept forward enough to give her fingers a quick lick, eyes never leaving Deke.

"It's okay, puppy," Deke said in his best critter voice, keeping his own hands flat on his thighs and leaning back in the couch. "I don't bite, and I sure hope you don't either."

"On your mat," Ellen said, snapping her fingers more sharply and pointing at the hearth rug. "Good girl."

Pebbles sat on the rug, tail switching arcs in the ash and splinters that always accompanied a wood stove in full use. She kept staring at Deke, something between a whine and growl squeaking out. But no hackles showed.

"Sorry about that," Ellen said, bending down to rub the dog's ears. "She's always been nervous around guys with beards. Not sure why, but she was nearly a year old when I got her from the shelter, so who knows what sort of childhood she had."

"That's all right," Deke said. "She doesn't have to come home with me or anything. Maybe I can win her heart with some more of Mrs. D's gingersnaps."

That laugh again. The one that set fire to his innards.

"*Please* don't," she said. "She'll barely be able to waddle up the stairs as it is."

Mrs. D came to door then, followed by the aromas of a full country spread. and even more molasses and spice.

"Y'all get on in here and dig in," she said, wiping her hands on her rag. "There's plenty for all, even that drainpipe named Fred. And I fixed a dab for Miss Pebbles, too."

That got the dog's eyes off of Deke. Pebbles was on her feet so fast he didn't see her move. She shot into the kitchen, hugging the wall farthest from Deke's feet, tail wagging so hard it was just a blur.

He laughed as he stood, holding his hand out to help Ellen to her feet.

"I reckon the fear of missing out beats the fear of the beard. Let's go get it while it's hot."

3

Lunch was a chorus of chatter, laughter, and clinking cutlery. And the occasional jowl-flapping belch from the corner where Pebbles plowed through more food than Ellen usually gave her in a week.

She hoped the coddled eggs and shredded chicken wouldn't mean a mess to clean up later, but trying to keep Grammy from foundering anything under her roof was a fool's errand.

With a groan, Deke pushed himself back from the overloaded table in defeat.

"Mrs. D, you're bound and determined to make me fat, I do believe."

She showed all her teeth and both dimples, patting his hand as she got up.

"Much work as you do for us, young man? I'd

have to cook twice as much before you had to unbutton your jeans."

Ellen saw an image that she hastily pushed out of her head. Or tried to, anyway.

Deke groaned again, which did nothing to help.

"No, Mrs. D. I'm serious. You're gonna kill me."

Grammy brought a pan of gingerbread to the table, along with about a pound of rich yellow butter from her friend Beulah's milk cow.

Pop's eyes lit up and he rubbed his hands together before taking up a knife and reaching for the pan.

"Yeah, but you'll die smilin'," he said, cutting four pieces that would probably be twelve servings on a nutrition label. "How much butter will you have, Ellie?"

She started to decline, then gave in. Nobody made gingerbread like Grammy. The coating of blue ribbons on the wall beside yonder wood stove was proof of that, if any was needed.

"Oh hell," she said. "Load me up, Pop. I can always get my old ten-speed out of the barn and ride it off."

Deke's protests had dried up, too. He took his own piece of decadence and dug in, closing his eyes and humming along to the sweet music of perfection.

"Can't nothin' fill a hole in the soul like your

Grammy's sweet ginger treats," Pop said, licking his lips and winking at the old lady. Grammy's face turned to fire and she popped him with her towel again as Deke tried to choke back a howl of laughter and only succeeded in spraying crumbs across the table.

Ellen wondered what ginger treats Deke might have to offer, and felt her own face heat up. Again. Good grief. She wasn't a teenager anymore.

Pop washed down the last of his own gingerbread with a big swig of milk (also courtesy of Beulah's cow) and set the glass down with a sigh of pure contentment.

"You doing the 'lectric for the G&B this year, Deke?"

"Mmm." Deke nodded and swallowed, then got his own drink to clear the sludge from his mouth. "Yessir. I got the gig for lights and sound, plus I'll be standing by for any booth repairs that need doing."

"Deke here is the best all-around handyman Green Cove has seen in quite a while," Grammy said, patting his hand. "I keep him in cookies, otherwise we'd never get any of his time."

"Speaking of time..." Deke checked his watch. "Mrs. D, I hate to leave while there's still food on your table, but I gotta run. Pete Stanley's fridge is on the blink, and Miss Quillen needs a ceiling fan hung.

Y'all need me to come by tomorrow morning to help you get all your goodies loaded up for the festival?"

"No, Deke. We'll have everything all Tupperwared and ready to go," Pop said, scootching his chair back and getting to his feet. "You one of the judges this year?"

Deke laughed again. He laughed a lot, and knew how to do it right.

Ellen wondered if she could learn how to make him laugh on cue, selfish reasons or not.

"Can't do it, Mr. D. I couldn't ever be fair and unbiased, not with Mrs. D's gingerbread and snaps on the table."

Now it was Deke's turn for a pop from the kitchen rag, but an awfully soft pop.

"You go on and get out of here, you flatterbug."

Today had been a day for laughter all around. Ellen wasn't sure when, but somewhere along the way her gloom had floated away on those gusts.

And she sure was glad.

4

———————

What a long day. Long, but fine as paint in Deke's opinion.

The vintage cuckoo clock hanging in his living room had just struck ten. The Daughtrys had their firewood, Pete's fridge sounded brand new, and Miss Quillen had her fan and was good to go.

He'd spent too long on the fan. Had to rewire it twice before he got the connections right. His mind had been on other things ever since that morning.

Things with long dark hair and darker eyes. Things with a laugh that punched him right in the gut.

Man, he hoped she'd like his surprise. Rather, that her dog Pebbles would. Making friends with poochie-poo couldn't hurt when it came to making friends with poochie-poo's mama. Besides, he liked dogs. Even watched a few when their own mamas and papas went away on vacation.

The sharp, warm scents of ginger and molasses filled the tiny apartment over Avery's Hardware. Not as scrumptious as what filled the Daughtry house, but a far cry from the usual cabbage soup or Mexican take-out he usually had at home.

The apartment didn't look much different from when he'd first moved in. Green linoleum with a typical Seventies geometric pattern of circles and octagons. Classic wood paneling that had hopefully gassed out the last of its formaldehyde a decade or two ago. Plain but comfortable rust-colored burlap couch and chair.

Be it ever so crumbled, there's no place like home.

Which wasn't really fair. Avery had let him repair the few odds and ends that needed it, even giving him the supplies from his stock downstairs.

Funny how he'd never noticed how boring the place was before. He tried to imagine bringing a lady friend here. Tried to see the apartment the way Ell... the way a woman might.

Maybe he should pick up a few throw pillows or something.

Never mind all that. He had a full day tomorrow and a couple of things left to do before bedtime.

Living above Main Street, he only had a couple of blocks' walk to the high school football field, which was already filling with pop-up awnings and long tables for tomorrow's Gingers and Breads festival.

He'd run most of the extension cords and power strips earlier that evening, and even borrowed one of those pillar-style propane heaters for Mrs. D's booth from Avery downstairs, with the promise to return it with a full tank after the festival.

His toolbox and belt sat by the door, ready for tomorrow's chores and fixits. On the red-and-chrome dinette table sat three containers that he hoped would make a decent showing.

He couldn't wait to see if they worked, even if he was a little nervous about the whole thing.

One final task before bed. One he hoped he remembered how to do after all these years.

Deke went into the bathroom. Turned on the light over the medicine cabinet. Laid the razor and cream he'd picked up on the way home on the edge of the sink.

He took one last look at his old self before sighing, picking up a pair of scissors, and starting to snip.

5

ELLEN HAD FORGOTTEN how much fun the Gingers and Breads festival could be.

The football field had been transformed into a snowy wonderland worthy of the North Pole. People dressed in sweaters even uglier than Pop's competed with jolly elves. A couple of adorable goofballs pranced around in polar bear costumes. There was even a White Witch, Narnia-style.

Endless loads of sugary ginger treats kept everyone spiked up and full of good cheer.

Tapped kegs of the local brew pub's hard ginger beer probably didn't hurt, either.

Two dozen tables and booths offered ginger candy, ginger milkshakes, ginger pudding, and several flavors of ginger ale of the softer variety.

There was even ginger ice cream, which was going fast in spite of the near-freezing temperatures.

And of course, there were gingersnaps, iced and nekkid. Gingerbread men, who had their own contest for best decorating. And good old-fashioned gingerbread squares. At least fifty different styles, most dolled up with fancy additions or exotic flavors.

But Grammy's booth had the longest line. Everyone in town wanted a piece of her traditional, tarry, blackstrap gingerbread. Ellen even heard one old biddy talking about how she'd taken an extra dose of insulin just for this.

Ellen and Pop sliced up square after square of Grammy's goodies, sticking a gingersnap in the center of each piece before handing it over to the next salivating sugar fiend in line while Grammy chattered and gossiped away. Pebbles, her leash clipped to a sturdy post driven into the ground, slept the sleep of sugar coma.

Ellen reminded herself to give Pebbles extra walkies later on. She dreaded what all those gingersnaps would do to pibble digestion.

"Seen Deke anywhere?" Pop asked around a mouthful of contraband gingersnap. "I figured he'd be makin' the rounds of the booths, checking for trouble."

Ellen didn't miss the side-eye he gave her.

Not that she'd been looking around for the handyman herself. Nope.

"I'm right here," said a familiar voice from the far side of the serving table. A voice that knew how to laugh.

"Why hell, I plumb didn't recognize you, Deke!"

Ellen looked up and recognized the green plaid flannel and the curly red hair. And those glacier-blue eyes, crinkled at the corners from a full-lipped smile unfettered by the mountain-man beard of yesterday.

"Hey, Mr. D, Mrs. D. Looks like the ginger-bread's a hit, as usual."

He spoke to her grandparents, but Deke looked straight into Ellen's eyes. She felt that same tingle light up her goosebumps and stir the coals in her belly.

"You look, um, different." Jesus, how lame was that? But he definitely did. His cheeks and chin were pale below the ruddier skin that hadn't been hidden by fur yesterday. Somehow the look worked on him. And on her.

"Yeah, well..." He rubbed a hand over his smooth face and laughed like he knew how. "Sure does feel weird. I haven't had a nekkid face in years. But you said as how Miss Pebbles there gets spooked by men with beards, so..."

Ellen heard a doggy *grrumph* and turned to see

Pebbles sitting up and staring at Deke, tilting her head first to one side, then the other. Sure, he *smelled* like the same guy and all, but...

This time Ellen laughed along with Deke like it was the most natural thing in the world.

"That reminds me," he said, reaching in his pocket and taking out a red tin box tied shut with a thin gold ribbon. "I got a present for Miss Pebbles. I hope she likes it."

He handed the box to Ellen. She pulled the ribbon free and opened it, revealing a small stack of dark brown, bone-shaped cookies.

"Gingersnap dog biscuits," Deke said, putting his hands in his pockets and scuffing one work-booted toe against the dirt. "I found a recipe on the internet. Supposed to be healthy for dogs. Healthier than people cookies, anyhow. Took me a bit of tinkering with some old stainless steel gutter flashing to get the bone shape right for the cutter, but I think they look okay."

"Well, I declare." Grammy said, coming over to inspect Deke's offering. "And just in time, too. Here comes Jack."

Jack Buchanan, Ellen's old mentor, walked up to Grammy's table wearing a Santa suit with a big purple button that read "JUDGE" in fancy gold script. His hair was thinner and whiter, and his back had a curve Ellen didn't remember. He'd gotten older since she'd been gone, but still had the cheerful and friendly smile he'd shown her so many times in the long-ago.

"I was just coming over to give Doreen her umpteenth blue ribbon," Jack said. "What's this I hear about dog biscuits? I'm afraid I wouldn't know how to judge those."

"We got us a fine judge right here, Jack," Pop said, plucking one of the biscuits from the box. Pebbles magicked to her feet, and Ellen was surprised she couldn't hear her tail whistle, it wagged so fast.

"Whatcha think, girlie?" Pop tossed the biscuit, and Pebbles came up on her hind feet to snatch it out of the air. Two quick crunches, and the canine gingersnap vanished.

Pebbles sat back down, maw gaping and tongue flapped out like a beach towel as she looked hopefully up at the box still in Ellen's hand.

"Well, I'd say that's settled then," Jack said, taking Deke's right hand and raising it high in the air. "Blue Ribbon for Best Ginger Dog Biscuits goes to Deacon Gantry!"

Everyone standing around the table broke into

cheers and applause. Deke grinned and looked down at his feet, while several people asked him to write down the recipe for their own pooches.

"What do you think?" Deke asked, glancing sideways at Ellen. "Think I might win her heart yet?"

Ellen noticed that her hand had somehow brushed against Deke's. She pulled it back, petted Pebbles's head instead.

"Maybe so," she said. "But I think you might need to give her a few more before she decides for sure."

Pop cleared his throat, breaking the Spell of Deke for the moment. She saw that he'd linked his fingers through Grammy's, and both of them were giving her...*looks*. Rather *sly* looks, at that.

"Deke, if you can tear yourself loose after the festival, why don't you come by the house after?" Pop said. "You can help me get Santa's sleigh up on the roof."

"And stay for dinner for your trouble, of course," Grammy said. "Maybe bring Miss Pebbles some more of those doggy biscuits for dessert."

"I'd be glad to," Deke said, still giving Ellen a look of his own. "If you don't think Miss Pebbles will mind the company."

"Speaking of," Jack said. He had a look on *his*

face too, dammit. Why was everyone *looking* at her today? "I might come by myself, if it's no trouble. I'd like to talk to you, Ellen. I'm meaning to retire this year or next, and I'm wondering if you might want to take on some of my clients once you get licensed in Virginia. You can paralegal for me in the meantime if you want. Keep your hand in."

That got Ellen's eyes off of Deke's.

"You mean you want me to take over your practice, Jack? Are you sure?"

"You have a fine mind for law, Ellen," he said. "And you have an even finer feel for people. Folks around here want someone they know handling their affairs. Or someone whose people they know. I think you can step right in with barely a ripple in the water."

Deke touched her shoulder, and she felt that zing again.

"This mean you might be staying in town a while? You and Miss Pebbles?"

Ellen looked from Jack, to Deke, to Pop, to Grammy. And back to Deke.

"Yeah," she said, feeling her smile bloom wide. "Yes. I think maybe I will."

"Well, that's all settled then," Grammy said, waving her arms at Pop and Jack. "Come on, you old fools. Let's us get on over to the ginger beer so these two can get it over with and smooch already."

Ellen wasn't sure who flamed hotter, her or Deke, but she was sure that together they gave off more heat than the propane fire.

She didn't even notice the whistles and cheers when Deke's lips finally met hers.

Laughing wasn't the only thing he knew how to do, after all.

Thank you for sharing your holidays with us!

Explore more from Jason's Brain Squirrel Garden at
www.JasonAdamsBooks.com

I hope you enjoyed reading the stories in *Winter Delights* as much as I enjoyed writing them.

Visit www.JasonAdamsBooks.com and join the adventure for exclusive new fiction, my past and future travels, and whatever else strikes my fancy. Hope to see you there!

Novellas:

Agonist

Collections and Anthologies:

Normally Fantastic

On the Case!

Capeless Heroes

Through the Squirrel Tree

Tales From the Squirrel Garden: Volume 1

(with Kari Kilgore)

Partnership in Crime

Shadows Mountain Deep

Partners in Romance

Near Future Forward

ABOUT JASON

Jason A. Adams writes across the spectrum. His stories include science fiction, fantasy, horror, Appalachian folk tales, and romance, of course.

You can find more of his work at www.JasonAdams-Books.com.

Jason's stories also appear in several issues of *Pulphouse Magazine, Mystery, Crime, and Mayhem, Uncollected Anthology, Thrill Ride,* and WMG Publishing's Holiday Spectaculars.

Jason, a recovering Air Force brat who grew up all over the US and Japan, now perches in the mountains of Southwest Virginia with his excellent author wife Kari Kilgore (www.karikilgore.com), several spoiled-rotten house critters, and assorted wild visitors from the nearby forest.

news@JasonAdamsBooks.com

A Huge Thank You to Our Amazing Kickstarter Backers!

This book wouldn't have happened without the people who believed in it. Y'all deserve a huge chunk of gratitude! None of you are getting coal in your stocking!

Unless you're a blacksmith. Then you deserve high-quality, low-sulfur coal, and lots of it!

Angela
Annie Reed
Anonymous Reader
Bob Clemens
Carolyn Rowland
Chris
Darth Wood
David H. Hendrickson
Dean Wesley Smith
Debbie Mumford
Dwayne Plain
Jean
Joe D'Agnese
Karen
Kat Tipton
Lady Catherine de Bourgh
Laura Ware

Lisa Silverthorne

Mary Jo Rabe

Meyari McFarland

Rebecca M. Senese

Ron Collins

Ryan M. Williams

Sean Monaghan

Stephania Carr

Sweetie Pie

The Salty B